Our Precious Earth

Emma Cameron

© 2024 Emma Cameron

ISBN 978-1-7385788-0-1

All rights reserved. No part of this publication may be reproduced, copied, stored in a retrieval system, or transmitted, by any form or in any means, without the prior written consent of the copyright holder, nor be otherwise circulated in any form of binding or cover other than that in which it is published and without a similar condition being imposed on the subsequent purchaser.

The author has asserted their moral right under the Copyrights, Designs and Patents Act 1988, to be identified as the author of their own work

A CIP catalogue record for this title is available from the British Library.

Published in the UK in 2024 by Emma Cameron

Cover design by Emma Ewbank

For Zephyr with love.

Acknowledgements

To earth defenders everywhere.

Thanks to Anna Hayward and Rob White for their support, the Bat Conservation Trust, Vincent Wildlife Trust and Sussex Bat Group for invaluable information, Emma Ewbank for the beautiful cover.

1

Ash's feet pressed into the soft earth. Sunlight flickered through the spaces between the trees – their branches covered in luminous green leaves – a time poised between Spring and Summer. Fox scat at the side of the path made her smile. A blackbird, calling urgently, flew from one tree to another; somewhere above a buzzard cried. A large blue-black beetle was lying on its back in the mud, legs waving in the air. Squatting down she righted it and watched as it scuttled away into the undergrowth.

She emerged from the wood by an old tree, known as the Whispering Oak, placing her hand on the trunk as she always did when passing. It was huge and sturdy – storm-scarred. Knots and bobbles covered the surface. Some of the outer bark had peeled off, brittle as hard leather; underneath was a landscape of swirls, like a Van Gogh painting. It was thought to be over five hundred years old, but no one knew for certain.

The oak was as wide as it was tall – the grass beneath was patterned by leaf shadows, creating a carpet of dark green and lime. Two hoverflies danced under the canopy, darting towards each other and then away, like two people on a first date.

Walking back across the field the sun warmed her bare shoulders. She joined the lane, walked for half a mile, before reaching her house, an end of terrace on the outskirts of Finsted. She climbed the steps and unlocked the door.

"Hello you two."

Tierre was sitting at the kitchen table with a schoolbook open, playing a game on her iPad. She looked up briefly. "Hi Mum."

Ash's partner, Jay, was cutting vegetables. The room was filled with the aroma of cumin.

"I'm making curry."

"Great, I'm starving."

She kissed them both, then flopped into a chair. That day she'd taken two parties of school students round the reserve to survey for invertebrates. It had been fun but exhausting. Part of her work at the wildlife trust was with young people, helping them to connect with nature. Sometimes, if they came from an urban area, they might take a while to engage, but then something – a bird, a particular flower, or an insect – sparked their interest. That day there'd been a girl who'd hung back, silent and unengaged, but Ash had talked to her and discovered she liked snakes. She'd shown her where they hid, under the corrugated iron sheets placed around the reserve and though they hadn't spotted any, the girl said she wanted to come back another time.

Tierre closed her iPad. "Can I go to Maya's at the

weekend? We're writing a play; her mum said we can borrow some clothes."

Maya was Tierre's closest friend. They'd known each other since year one. Her mum, Grace, was an actor and had a wardrobe of extravagant clothes and accessories that she was happy to let them use.

"Of course. What's the play about?"

"There are four people on a broken-down boat in the middle of the ocean, they try to make friends with the dolphins, so they'll pull them to safety. The dolphins are suspicious, they think the people might want to eat them."

Tierre loved the sea and everything that lived in it.

"It sounds brilliant."

"It will be."

"How was work?" she asked Jay.

"Good. We finished the contract and they were happy, so we should get paid soon."

Jay's website design company that he ran with his friend Ranil had its ups and downs but right now was going well.

The curry was delicious. Jay, when he had time and the inclination, was a great cook. After eating they settled down on the sofa. Tierre leant in close to Ash.

"Have you seen this?" Jay said, passing Ash his phone.

She read what was on the screen.

The Roads Agency press release: Bypass route announced.

"I thought that was tomorrow."

The orange route has been chosen for the missing link of the A27. This could save commuters an hour each week and keep the impact on the national park to a minimum.

"I don't believe it! They can't have chosen that route. *Keep the impact to a minimum,* that's a lie. What about the green route? It's so much less destructive. F…" She was going to swear then remembered she was trying not to around Tierre, so she got up and went out into the garden. Jay followed her.

"It's madness."

"What about the wildlife, the bats and foxes and badgers that'll be killed crossing the road. How can they let that happen? It's just wrong," she said.

The bats would be out soon, swooping down to the pond for the first insects of the night. Unaware of what lay ahead. Ash sighed deeply.

"That route will destroy part of the wood." Then she remembered. "The oak, the Whispering Oak, they'll fell it. They can't do that."

She looked at Jay.

"I know how much it means to you."

"It mustn't happen."

He put his arms round her. "It'll be OK."

"Will it?"

"Come on, let's go inside."

Tierre was looking worried.

"Are you alright Mum?"

"I'm a bit upset, sweetheart, it's a shock."

Tierre picked up her stuffed dolphin from the sofa.

"Swimmy says she'll keep the animals safe."

*

Later when Tierre had gone to bed, Ash said, "I'm

going down to the moon pond."

Jay looked up from his laptop. "Do you want me to come?"

"No, it's OK."

She walked half a mile down the lane, past the vicar, Hazel's, house. The light was on, and she saw the tall figure walking across the room, wondered if she was lonely. Joanna, her partner, was often away on archaeological digs.

It was a still evening. The moon pond was catching the last light from the sky. She stood on the bank, fitted the detector into her phone and turned on the app. The light faded and she heard the call of a tawny owl, echoed by its mate. She was suspended in that space; a world where ordinary life and human noise disappeared. The darkening line of the hawthorn hedge stretched down to the woods. Midges and craneflies floated above the pond and small creatures rustled in the tall grass and nettles behind.

A tiny shape flitted across her eyeline. The detector came alive, red fizzing audio graphs on the screen, and a series of short sounds and clicks – a cross between a robin's alarm call and a distant sputtering scooter. The calls grew louder and then faded. A larger shape flicked across her vision, then another; on and on they came, from all directions, the detector telling her the species – Daubenton's, Common Pipistrelles, Noctule, Brown Long Eared bat.

Echolocation enabled them to find their way their prey in the dark, making rapid twists and turns to pluck the moths and midges from the air. The sounds were like an ancient secret language – if she was reverent and quiet, she might be allowed to move through a portal into their bat space.

The world was alive under her feet and above her head. The mud and the earth teemed with life, with worms, beetles, woodlice, spiders and above her head were the clouds, the stars, the wind, the moon, the perfection of night. The last of the light faded in the west. A new moon was rising and close by a planet; Jupiter she thought.

She walked home, keeping the torch low so as not to disturb any creatures. The road would go across the fields not far from here. There would be lights, noise, fast cars and motorbikes at war with animal routes and rhythms. The creatures and, ultimately, they would lose.

2

A week after the announcement about the bypass there was a meeting in the village hall. Their MP and a representative from the Roads Agency would be there to give more information and to take questions.

"I'm going, I need to find out what's happening," Ash said.

"OK, I'll stay with Tierre."

"I don't need babysitting," Tierre protested.

"No, but your mum can tell us what they say," Jay said.

When she arrived, the hall was full. She greeted several people she knew, including George, the usually cheerful pub manager, who just nodded and said, "Bad day."

On the wall was a large map showing the possible routes of the bypass, coloured blue, green and orange. She studied it. The route that had been chosen went south of the village, crossing the field where the Whispering Oak stood, passing close to the church, straddling the chalk stream and skirting the school in Westerden. From the diagram it was clear that the Whispering Oak, along with several others in the south-west corner of the wood, would disappear.

The blue route passed close to the village of Thornton. The green route was an upgrade of an existing road and would be the least damaging.

Someone called, "We're ready to start." Ash found a seat at the back of the room.

The Chair, Councillor Beth Giles, introduced the two men sitting on either side of her, MP Richard Netherley and John Slant from the Roads Agency. "As you're aware a decision has been reached. I'll leave it to our MP to tell you more, then there'll be time for questions."

Richard Netherley stood up. He'd been her MP for several years and she disagreed with most of what he said. A Tory. He was large, middle aged, round face, with thinning hair, wearing a shirt and blue tie. He had the posture and air of someone who'd never known poverty or struggle.

"Good evening. Thank you all for coming. As you may be aware, after very careful consideration, the orange route has been chosen for the bypass. This meeting is to address any concerns."

Voices called out, "That route is at the end of my garden." "What about noise pollution?" "My kids are at that school."

The Chair said, "Please. We will take questions one at a time." Hands went up. "The woman there." She pointed towards Mrs Burnett, who was sitting in the row in front of Ash.

Mrs Burnett lived in a cottage on Sheep Lane, close to the woods. She stood up, using a stick and said in a shaky voice, "I've been told my house is condemned, what will happen to me? I'm too old to move."

Netherley looked taken aback, as if he wasn't expecting someone so elderly to be there.

"Well Mrs....?

"Burnett."

"Mrs Burnett. You'll be offered compensation and time to find another home that's suitable for you. You'll receive a very generous offer. I'm sure you'll be more than happy with it. I hope that reassures you. Shall we have the next question?"

Ash was shocked at how dismissive he was. The old woman sat down looking confused and upset. Ash put a hand on her shoulder and whispered, "So sorry."

A man stood up. "The road passes right next to the school my two kids are at, what about the noise and pollution?'

"I'll let Mr Slant from the Roads Agency answer that one," Netherley said.

"Thank you for the question. Rest assured, a large fence will be erected to screen out noise and fumes in sensitive areas such as this. The road won't be visible and will hardly be heard."

"You can't screen out fumes...." The man said.

"Sorry, we only have time for one question, next person," the Chair pointed to a woman in the middle.

Questions and concerns were dismissed or answered with platitudes. Ash, who'd had her hand up for a while and been ignored, couldn't contain herself any longer and stood up.

"My name's Ash Morton, I'm a naturalist. As well as all the issues raised, the orange route means the felling of the Whispering Oak. It's an ancient tree and it's precious, as is the rest of the wood. You'll destroy a whole ecosystem."

Netherley answered immediately and seemed well prepared for what she was saying. "Please sit down, Ms Morton. According to new research the tree is not as old as has been proclaimed. It is in fact only around two hundred and fifty years old."

A lie, said with confidence, was still a lie. She refused to be intimidated.

"Can you tell me where you got that information, please?"

"You'll have to take my word for it, I'm afraid."

She could sense his animosity, even though she was standing way back, but she persisted.

"There are bats in the area, some of them rare, such as Barbastelles; it will destroy their habitat."

"We don't have time for a long debate, Ms Morton. Please put any complaints in writing."

John Slant stood up and began telling them about proposals for planting new trees along the route, for sound mitigation and rehoming the dormouse population. It might fool some people but not her. She'd heard enough. She slipped out the back of the hall.

There was a pain in her lower stomach, maybe the beginning of her period, though it wasn't quite due. She leant against the wall, bent over. She imagined the road howling through the countryside like a demented beast, erasing the oak, Mrs Burnett's cottage, scattering badgers and foxes, obliterating the chalk stream.

Walking home, noticing the quiet and the evening light illuminating the creamy hawthorn flowers in the hedgerow. An early bat, maybe a noctule, swept over her head, along the lane, towards the wood.

That night she dreamt she was trapped inside the oak tree; half of the trunk had fallen away, it was rotting at the core, an invisible cancer, like the one that killed her mum. She was trapped and couldn't escape, there was a feeling of terror. She woke herself up, but the dream was hard to shake off. She moved close to Jay, needing to feel his body.

*

Finsted village consisted of around sixty houses, scattered along three lanes. It had a church, the village hall and one pub.

Ash, Jay and Tierre lived in a row of ex-council houses on the western edge of the village. Ash had been born in Thornton, on the other side of the common, close to the wood. The area was in her blood, her heart was in the chalk, the white paths snaking over the Downs; the hillsides in protected areas producing displays of wildflowers each Spring and Summer, like the palette of an Elizabethan embroidery, gold, white, pink, blue, lavender. Her connection to nature was central to her life, a core of strength. It saw her through difficult times, the loss of her mother, a lover leaving, the death of a close friend in a car accident.

She'd been an only child, like Tierre. The creatures she met were her friends, the fox with four cubs at the end of the garden, the hedgehogs, the badgers who built their setts in the muddy banks. She learned the rhythms of the seasons, waited impatiently for the snowdrops, watching for the primroses and white stars of the wood anemones, scattered like snowflakes over the ground, revelling in the bluebells and inhaling the scent of wild garlic. She learned to listen for the birds, the first chiff chaff, the distinctive song of the song thrush, cheery robins, beautiful blackbirds, tuneful blackcaps and willow warblers. She looked out for the small creatures too, the spiders and wood lice, the speckled wood butterflies flitting in and out of sunny spots.

Aged six she'd found a bat huddled in the corner on the doorstep. A tiny reddish-brown thing. Most likely a Pipistrelle she knew now. Mum had found a box for it and given it some water and said they would keep it safe until dusk, then try releasing it. They'd waited and waited; she'd wanted to keep looking in the box but Mum said it was best to leave it alone. When the time came the bat had hesitated, clutching on to Mum's gloved hand, shivering as if excited or scared, and then stretched out its delicate, strong wings and flown away, zipping fast over the fence, disappearing into the dark night. It was the moment she knew what to do with her life. She learned all she could about bats and discovered there were some she could hear. People always said that was impossible; now she knew it had probably been a brown long-eared bat, whose calls had a lower frequency.

She'd gone north to university and then to Europe to study, but it was only when she planted her feet on the chalk and the springy grass that she felt at home.

*

It was thought that the Whispering Oak had been given its name because people whispered their secrets to it. There were local stories of assignations and betrayals under the tree. One of the most powerful was about a young woman who climbed the oak to escape her violent father and, just as he was about to catch her, a large branch fell on his head, killing him.

Ash's Mum had her own tale. She'd really wanted a child but after trying for three years they were beginning to give up hope. One hot day in summer Mum had told her story to the tree, then lain down underneath it and fallen asleep. She'd dreamed of a jay planting an acorn. A few weeks later she discovered she was pregnant. Dad always laughed when she told the story. "Are men redundant now, Cathy?"

When Mum died, they scattered her ashes at the base of the tree. Although they'd long ago merged with the earth, Ash still felt her spirit in that place.

3

Sunlight glowed through the stained glass, throwing blue and red light onto the ochre tiles where she was sitting. Ash wasn't religious but the bats roosting in the tower made the church a hallowed place.

Hazel appeared from the chantry, startling her.

"Hello Ash. How are you? I don't often see you in here."

"Hi Hazel. I wanted a place to think. I'm still trying to take in the news about the bypass."

"It's hard to believe they chose that route." Hazel came and sat on the pew next to her. "It will pass so close to the church. I'm worried about the pollution and the vibration of the traffic on the foundations. The frescoes too – when Joanna uncovered them five years ago, she said we must protect them."

"We have to do something," Ash said, looking at the central window for inspiration. It depicted a line of pilgrims carrying large sacks, bent under their weight. Her own metaphorical burden was knowing the truth about their rapidly heating world.

"It means a lot to you, I know." Hazel put a hand on her arm.

"I was born here, I'm protective of the land, we can't allow them to destroy everything."

"They've been pushing for this for a long time and many people want the bypass, so they don't have to sit in traffic. It will take a lot to stop it."

"There must be a way."

Hazel was quiet for a minute then said, "Well… you have a lot of knowledge and passion. You could start a campaign."

Ash occasionally went on a march but had never organised a protest. She was a dreamer, a nature lover, never happier than when reading the latest research on animal ways, like recently when scientists discovered that bats sing to each other. She'd been quiet at school, not wanting to reveal her real passions which were for nature and wild creatures, particularly the less attractive ones, rather than music and fashion like the other girls.

"I don't know… maybe."

"Well, think about it. You'd have my support."

*

After her conversation with Hazel, Ash began talking to people she met about the bypass. Most people in the village were upset but appeared resigned to the idea that it would happen. Some, like her immediate neighbours, Paula and David, said, "Sorry Ash, the route will save us time – we support it."

In town people seemed enthusiastic. Conversations in shops were, "At last, we've been waiting for this for years." "The sooner they build it the better."

Two weeks later the town council passed a resolution supporting the orange route. The wealthiest landowner in the area was known to be a keen advocate and Netherley was determined it would go ahead. Ash realised that people were being driven by their desire for comfort and were still unaware how fragile the nature they all depended on had become.

At work she talked to her friend Beccy, who lived in town but was a passionate advocate for nature.

"The vicar said I should lead a campaign."

"Good idea. Are you going to?"

Ash shrugged. "I don't know if I'm the best person, I'm not very good at speaking out but I can't just sit and watch it happen."

"Then do it. I'd love to be involved but Mum's dementia is getting worse, looking after her is hard. I'll help as much as I can, I can do social media."

"That's a start. Let's arrange a meeting and maybe start a WhatsApp group. We need to get people together."

*

Ash found Jay and Tierre watering pots in the garden.

"I've decided to start a campaign against the bypass."

"OK, just you?" Jay said.

"Beccy and Hazel said they'd help; we're having a meeting on Saturday to get more support. Can you come?"

He filled the watering can and gave it to Tierre who poured it over a pot of blue geraniums.

"I'm cycling with Danny."

"You didn't tell me."

"Sorry I thought I had. You're at Maya's, aren't you Tierre?"

"Yeah." Tierre ran down the garden and jumped the width of the pond. "Have we finished?"

"Sure, thanks for helping."

"You do care about the bypass, don't you?"

"You know I do. I'll come to the next one."

*

They met at the village hall. The map showing the route was still on display. Ash had a strong desire to rip it from the wall. Despite the short notice ten people turned up, more than she'd expected. Mrs Burnett wasn't one of them and Ash hoped she wasn't ill.

Ash said, "Thanks everyone for coming. I'm not used to chairing meetings, but I think if we introduce ourselves and say how the road will affect us, that would be a start. Beccy will take notes. Is that OK?"

They nodded.

A man sitting next to her introduced himself as Mark, and said, "My son has just started at the local school. When the bypass is finished, he'll have to cross the road by the bridge, it's going to make their journey longer and more difficult."

Liz, an older woman, who she knew by sight, spoke next. "The road will pass the end of my garden. I'll hear it day and night."

Hazel talked about her concerns for the structure of the old church and disturbance to the graveyard.

Ash explained the importance of the area's ecosystem, the ancient oak and the wildlife that would be affected by the road, the dormice population, wild birds and the many species of bats.

Voice after voice expressed their concerns.

The last person to speak was a young woman called Dora. She was tall, slender, with short, flame-coloured hair. She spoke with a tremor in her voice.

"We live near the route in Westerden. My younger sister, Holly, is asthmatic. We moved here from London because she kept having attacks. She hasn't had one for two years now, Mum is worried it will start again if they build the road."

People shook their heads and murmured sympathetically.

"It's clear from what everyone has said that the road will have a devastating effect on the area. Let's go round again and think of all the things we can do to stop it," Ash said.

Beccy said she'd set up a social media account. Mark suggested starting a petition. Dora said she would write a letter to the local paper. Liz said she would put an article on her writer's blog to raise awareness of the issues. Ash said she would write to Richard Netherley.

The room was full of energy and enthusiasm as they collected the ideas and at the close of the meeting, people thanked Ash for bringing them together.

Hazel stayed behind to help put the chairs away. "You did well, Ash."

"I'm happy to be doing something, I feel more hopeful now."

She walked home, thoughts about what to do next buzzing in her head.

When Jay got back from his ride she hugged him.

"You're in a good mood," he said.

"It was a great meeting, lots of ideas, we just need to put them into action now. How was your ride?"

"Brilliant, we did sixty miles up to Box Hill and back. I sweated buckets, I'm going for a shower."

*

Ash was writing a letter to Netherley, detailing all their concerns. She was trying to make it sound rational and coherent and to keep her emotion out of it.

"Mum, can you help me? I don't understand this homework," Tierre said.

She didn't like maths and often wanted Ash to explain things, knowing she'd have the answers.

"Can you wait a little, sweetheart? I just need to finish this email."

"OK."

"You're working hard," Jay said.

She looked up. "I'm writing to Netherley – I need to do it tonight."

"So long as you don't forget us."

She gave him a look to show her annoyance but didn't say anything, not wanting to upset Tierre, who hated it if they argued. He went back to his laptop.

*

The action group agreed that Hazel's suggestion, to organise a walk along the route of the proposed bypass, was a good one. The aim was to show which houses would be most affected and help people understand more about the area's ecosystem. Ella, Ash's boss, who knew the area well, had agreed to lead it.

They met outside the church. There was about thirty people and, to her surprise, Netherley was one of them. He was with a smartly dressed young woman, who she assumed was his assistant. Ash glanced at him, ready to say hello, but he looked straight through her.

Ella gathered them together and said, "We're here to show you how the bypass will affect this area. St Nicholas's church is 12th century. The road will pass across there." She pointed to the bottom of the slope, below the graveyard. "As well as the noise pollution and disruption during the construction, the bats that roost in the tower will be affected; we have fourteen kinds in the area, several are rare. They use the hedgerows as navigation aids; the lights will disorient them, traffic can kill them and some of their roosting sites will be destroyed." There was murmuring. "Right, we'll continue along the route."

They walked down the lane. Ella pointed out the hedges. "These hedgerows are an important habitat for wildlife, nesting birds, spiders, insects, mice and voles. The road means these will go." She gestured behind her. "The line of trees you can see on the other side of this field will be felled. There will be a viaduct eight metres high going across the horizon line."

Ash sensed a current of shock go round the group. She already knew about the viaduct.

"That's terrible, I can't imagine anything that high,"

one of her neighbours, Kay, said.

Others said, "The view will change completely." "How can they even think about it?"

People huddled together, murmuring, looking distressed and upset.

Ella said, "Let's move to the wood now and Ash will talk to you about the oak trees."

They stood under the Whispering Oak.

Ash said, "This tree, called the Whispering Oak, is one of several ancient trees in the area. It's hugely important. Oaks live a long time. They sustain thousands of insects, invertebrates, birds, mammals and wild plants. They also accumulate a rich history. Imagine everything it has witnessed, life, love, death and birth, it's part of the history of this community. It isn't just any tree, it's a storyteller, a counsellor, a feeder for wildlife and for our souls." She stopped; aware she was talking a lot. "We need to protect it and the rest of the wood."

Netherley, who, up to then had been quiet, said, in a voice cracking with impatience, "It's just one tree, many more will be planted along the route."

"You can't replace an ancient tree, it takes hundreds of years to establish an ecosystem," Ash said.

He stared at her with a look of dislike and said, "We must have progress."

His assistant was typing into her phone. He turned to her and said, "No need to take that down."

Ash resisted the strong urge to continue arguing with him, knowing it wasn't the right place for it.

They walked on and joined Sheep Lane, arriving

at two houses close together. The first was Walnut Tree Cottage, a small flint house with a neat front garden. There were several birdfeeders hanging from a tree, which were covered in blue tits, chaffinches and sparrows.

"Mrs Burnett has lived here for over fifty years. It's going to be demolished, as is the one next to it," Ash said.

Netherley had moved closer to her. "This is a very isolated place; perhaps she would benefit from being nearer other people?"

Ash said, "It's her home. She loves this garden and the birds."

The atmosphere between them was thick with dislike. They were standing under a large beech tree. At that moment Ash noticed a crow with two white feathers hopping along a branch. She recognised it as one she sometimes gave peanuts to – it had learnt to catch them its beak. The crow dropped shit on the arm of Netherley's jacket. He cursed and looked up, a furious expression on his face. The bird flew away.

Ash smiled to herself. Corvids were very intelligent – they remembered the people who harmed them and those who helped them.

The walk ended back at the church. Netherley thanked Ella; he didn't look at Ash.

4

They stood in front of a small painting of a tree in full leaf, a blue sky, the grass beneath dotted with white flowers. Above the tree floated a figure in a pale lemon dress. The detail, when Ash looked closer, was extraordinary. The colours were bright and fresh, as if they'd just been painted. The exhibition in a local gallery was of work by artists who'd at one time lived or worked in Sussex.

"This one's beautiful," Ash said.

Jay looked at the label. "It's called Clara and the Oak. That's a coincidence, it says the artist lived near Finsted for a few years."

"It's like a younger Whispering Oak. I wonder who Clara was?" Ash said.

"She looks like an angel," Tierre said.

The artist was a visionary and a poet. Ash imagined him wandering the lanes and fields, passing the oak, at that time only two hundred and fifty years old, in a floppy hat and felt breeches, stooping to enter the cottage where his wife would be baking or helping the children. The painting was a tribute to his daughter Clara, who'd died of pneumonia aged fifteen. Ash imagined her as a girl who wanted to climb trees, pleading with her father, "Papa, please lift me up." He would oblige and she'd pull herself up, put her leg over the branch and soon be sitting astride. She'd sit smiling, looking down on her father and her younger brother who was calling to her to come down.

Maybe, wanting to honour her and remember her happiness, the artist had painted her as an angel, flying over the canopy. Ash imagined him in despair and grief, leaning into the oak, finding comfort in the enormous strength of the trunk and heft of the limbs.

"The tree is holding her up, so we can't let it die," Tierre said.

"I won't let anything happen to the tree," Ash said.

*

Tierre would be thirteen in August. She was her own person, shy, friendly, serious, playful and loved the sea. They lived two miles from the coast and the sea was part of their lives. There were photos of her as a baby sitting in the shallows, smiling with delight as the ripples touched her bare toes.

Ash went to say goodnight. The bedroom was small, but everything fitted in, shelves up one wall, for books and things she'd collected from the beach, an orange crab shell, a smooth fork-shaped piece of wood, a mermaid's purse; there was a chest of drawers, a pinboard for photos. There was one of her and Maya, dressed up in feather boas, one pink, one red, laughing and posing for the camera. Until a year ago she'd slept with Swimmy, then it was discarded – recently it had taken up residence again.

Her daughter was sitting up in bed, her pale face illuminated by the bedside light.

"Mum – are we all going to die?"

Ash sat on the bed. "What's happened?"

"That's what he said."

"Who?"

"Mr Roberts. The geography teacher. The planet will soon be too hot for us to live in."

Tierre turned her head to the wall, ran a nail down the paint, making a line in the turquoise, a chip under her fingernail, which she picked out.

Ash hoped the teacher hadn't said that. "It's true that the planet is getting hotter, but there's still time to turn it around."

"I'm frightened."

Ash put her arms around her daughter.

"I'll do everything I can to help make the world a safe place, I promise."

"But you're not in charge."

Ash pulled her closer. "Who says? It will be OK. You mustn't worry." She knew as soon as she said it that telling someone not to worry didn't work. "There are things we can do. The campaign to stop the bypass will help, and you've got me, your dad and Maya, your other friends; you're not alone."

"Will you stay with me until I go to sleep?"

"Of course."

Tierre lay down. Ash pulled the duvet up and

stroked her hair. Soon her eyes closed and her breathing became more regular.

Ash turned out the light and tiptoed out of the room.

Jay was watching TV.

"Tierre says she's scared about what's happening to the climate, her geography teacher said something really negative."

He muted the sound. "We can't help what she hears at school."

"No but I keep thinking there's something else we should be doing."

"Help her to take her mind off it. It's not good to dwell on things. Let's go to the beach this weekend, we could take Maya too."

"I wonder how many other young people feel like this."

"You worry too much, come here and have a hug."

*

Ash first realised her daughter was upset about what was happening to the world a few years earlier. Tierre had come home from school with a drawing of a brightly coloured bird. Underneath she'd written, "Blue Throated Macaw of Bolivia."

"What a beautiful picture."

"Ms Jeffries let us choose which one to draw, there were five animals, one was a polar bear, nearly everyone chose that or a tiger, but I like this bird, it's so colourful. The teacher said they only live in one place on earth and there aren't many left. Why are so many things dying?"

Ash had known this conversation would come but still wasn't prepared for it.

"It's true that some animals and plants are disappearing, but others are coming back, like the otters. Many people are trying to take care of the forests where the parrots live but there are companies who want to cut down trees to grow crops. I hope we can save the blue macaw."

It didn't seem an adequate explanation but when Tierre had finished eating, she left the drawing on the table and went to play outside. Later Ash asked if she wanted to talk more about the parrot but Tierre shook her head.

*

Ash hadn't planned to get pregnant. She was twenty-eight when it happened which still gave her plenty of time to decide whether to have children or not. Although she wanted a child, she was aware that things were not right with the world; the Amazon jungle was being deforested, there were wars, nature was under threat – she didn't know if it was right to bring a child into a world full of uncertainty.

Jay had been keen and persuaded her it would be OK. He was a good father and despite her doubts Ash thought she'd made the right decision.

Tierre had planted her feet on the earth, wide-eyed, with a determination that was almost unnerving. She was open with them; told them of worries about her looks, was her nose too big? [no, it's perfect], about her friends being mean, [sometimes people take their hurts out on each other] about teachers who were harsh [do you want me to say something to him?].

Ash hated the idea of her daughter being frightened. As adults, it was their responsibility to look after the earth and mostly they were failing. It made her even more determined to stop the bypass, to show Tierre that they had the power to change things.

*

Beccy was good with graphics and designed an eye-catching flyer, detailing all the negative impacts of the road. Ash, Liz and Beccy handed them out in the town centre on a Saturday afternoon. When people saw the headline, No Finsted Bypass, many of them shook their heads, ignoring the proffered leaflet. Others were more sympathetic and stopped to sign the petition. They collected over a hundred signatures in a day.

The Stop the Bypass group, as they'd decided to call themselves, had agreed to talk to as many of their neighbours as possible to get support for the campaign.

The fields to the south of the wood were owned by the Fullers, whose farm was on Long Lane. It was known that the farm wasn't doing well. Neither Andrew nor Christine Fuller had been to the meeting and Ash was certain they supported the road, even though it went through their land.

Despite living in the same village for the past fifteen years she rarely saw them. They had two boys, a teenager at the same school as Tierre, Gavin, and an older boy, Liam. Andrew Fuller drove too fast along the lanes. He sometimes drank at the local pub but she didn't think he had any friends there.

Ash knocked on the door of the farmhouse. A dog barked loudly inside.

Someone opened an upstairs window and called, "Who is it?"

She stepped back and looked up. The face at the window was Christine Fuller's.

"Hi, it's Ash Morton, can I talk to you for a minute? It's about the bypass."

"I'm busy right now."

"The road cuts right across your land, what will happen to the farm?"

Christine Fuller shrugged. "That's not a problem for us, sorry I need to go." She shut the window.

Ash turned away and walked down the drive to the gate. Outside, Gavin was sitting on a log, kicking at the gravel.

She said hello.

He didn't look up but as she passed, he said, "You like bats, don't you?"

She turned. "I love them. Why?"

"We've got bats, I see them at night in the yard, they're cool."

"I've got a great bat detector, you plug it into a phone, it's amazing. I could show you sometime."

He gave a half smile, then said, "I don't want to leave."

"Oh. Have you told them that?"

He shrugged, pulled his knees, skinny in the faded jeans, up to his chin.

"No point, they don't listen."

She said goodbye, wondering about him; he seemed lonely.

5

In early June there was an announcement that work would begin on construction of an access road for the bypass. On a very hot day Ash stood under the Whispering Oak. She shaded her eyes from the sun and looked out across the common. If the road went ahead, where she was standing would be the central reservation. Every leaf, root and branch would turn to concrete and tarmac. She was aware of a deep sorrow, an ancient yearning for a time when humans were an equal part of the natural world, no more or less than any other beings, instead of the omnipotent beasts they'd become. She made a promise to the tree that she would do everything in her power to protect it.

Later she phoned her dad to tell him about the bypass, somehow thinking he might be upset because of Mum's ashes, but all he said was, "There's nothing much you can do about that, is there?"

She was annoyed by the resignation in his voice, but then he'd never been a fighter.

After Mum died twenty years earlier, he'd moved

to Dorset and married Lydia, a very different woman, who liked long holidays and dining out. Although he was fond of Tierre, they didn't see much of him.

Ash had been in her second year at university when Mum was diagnosed with ovarian cancer. They hadn't told Ash straight away, not wanting to disrupt her studies, and by the time she returned home for the summer the cancer had advanced. Chemotherapy hadn't worked and there was no further treatment. Ash had been furious at them for not telling her earlier, but the anger soon gave way to grief.

She'd been aiming to go travelling with a friend but instead stayed at home for the summer. They'd talked, whenever Mum had the energy. She said of course she didn't want to die but she'd had fifty-two years on the earth which was more than many people had. She was going back to be with her beloved nature, where she belonged. Ash had somehow been reassured by her acceptance of death. During the last two weeks of her life, in early July, they moved her bed to the downstairs room and left the door open to the garden so she could hear the birdsong. She'd died at night, when Ash was sleeping; Dad said she was very peaceful.

Mum's face was becoming indistinct in Ash's mind but her voice, a high soprano, was still alive and present. One of her favourite songs, a West Country folk song, Where the Old Oak Grows, that she'd sung around the house, often popped into Ash's head.

*

Ash was born in 1978, the year before Margaret Thatcher came to power.

Some of her earliest memories were of the fear around the threat of nuclear war, overheard from her parents' whispered conversations, along with snippets and phrases from radio and television - the Cold War, the Iron Curtain, the grim and powerful images – ice, blood and snow. Barbed wire, snipers, metal gates clanging shut.

Cruise Missiles came to the UK. Primed and pointing. She understood that it could mean a terrible war, the end of days. She imagined a kind of blackness, with nothing around, or beyond. Lying awake, eyes squeezed shut, trying to block out the horrible thoughts in her mind.

One night she sat on the stairs and listened to her parents talking, Dad's voice sharp. "You promised you wouldn't, it might be dangerous, you could be arrested, what about Ashley?" She was called that back then.

"I have to, Ed, don't you see, what kind of future will she have if there's a nuclear war?"

After that Mum went away for a while. Greenham Common, she found out later. Dad had taken her to school, holding her hand very tight, as if she might run away too. When Mum returned, she seemed different and separate, less just a mum, more of a mystery – empowered, Ash would describe it as now.

At university Ash studied ecology, then spent a year abroad, visiting the forests of Eastern Europe, looking for the elusive lynx, for vultures and wolves. Spending long hours in a hide on the sides of a gorge, with binoculars, listening for the crackle of a footstep in the undergrowth, a distant call, distinctive stripes on a wing, a soaring, majestic shape in the sky. Visiting remote caves to study bat populations, gazing in wonder at the clouds of creatures emerging at dusk.

In her late twenties there was a drip, drip of articles about melting glaciers and icecaps; photographs of polar bears clinging onto rapidly dwindling ice, unable to hunt; forests burning, along with the creatures that lived in them. The Amazon was being cleared of its magnificent trees to make space for agriculture, Indigenous lands and lives being lost. There were too many greenhouse gases in the atmosphere, the world was heating up.

The cruise missiles had gone but the climate was being turned into a weapon – no-one knew where it would strike next.

*

Jay and Tierre had gone for an early cycle ride. Ash was jolted awake by a heavy vehicle which shook the house as it passed.

She got up, dressed and hurried down the lane in the direction of the sound. As she got closer, she could see a lorry and several people standing by the wide hedgerow that bordered the edge of a field. The hedge was a joy, a mixture of blackthorn and hawthorn, wide and long. It was covered in white blossom in spring and there were berries in autumn, a feast for birds and other wildlife. There weren't many like it left in the area.

As she got closer, she saw one of the men lift a

chainsaw and fire up the engine. Fear gripped her and she began to run. By the time she reached them he'd started cutting.

"Stop, there are birds nesting," she shouted.

The man cut the engine and held up his hand. "Don't come any nearer. It's dangerous."

She could hear the distressed call of small birds.

"You can't cut the hedge, you'll kill them."

"Sorry, it's not our problem, you'll have to take it up with the Roads Agency."

The other men were watching, but none intervened.

"The sparrows have young chicks. It's illegal to cut a hedge in nesting season," Ash said.

"We've been given the go ahead," he said, restarting the machine.

"Please, stop," she begged, trying to get closer but the others barred her way.

Not knowing what to do, she called Jay but his phone went straight to voicemail. She tried Dora.

"They're cutting down the hedge by the wood."

"God that's awful, sorry I can't get there, can you stop them?"

"They won't let me get near, it's terrible."

"Take photos if you can, so we've got evidence."

Ash cut the call and began filming, trying to hold the phone steady though her hands were shaking.

Sawing, cutting, flaying, destroying, the men hurled branches, leaves and, she was sure, nests, into the chopping machine. The adult birds were calling loudly. Ash was filming and crying. The destruction felt visceral, as if it was an abuse of her own body, a cutting of flesh, a wounding of her soul.

After a while her phone ran out of power, and she could only watch. They stopped when there was half the hedge left.

"Please leave the last part," she shouted.

The man with the chainsaw shouted, "Sorry can't do that," and after a few moments restarted the machine. They soon reached the end of the now-silent, flayed hedge. She was hollowed out with shock and grief, for the parents and young birds and the loss of the beautiful habitat. She walked away, hating them and everything that was happening to the world. The sparrows were tiny precious creatures, on the red list of endangered birds – the loss was tragic.

When she got home Jay and Tierre were eating breakfast.

"We thought you were still asleep," Jay said.

She went to the sink for a glass of water, unable to speak.

"What's wrong, Mum?"

She told them, almost choking on the words.

"They destroyed the hedge – the one in the field where the sparrows nest. I felt like I was witnessing a murder."

"Why did they do that?" Tierre asked.

"I don't know, they said they're clearing the way for an access road."

"We can write and complain," Jay said.

"It won't bring the hedge back. It's criminal."

"I suppose it means they're going to start construction."

She stood looking out of the window at the small wild garden. She was cold, although it was a warm day.

"Can we still go to the beach?" Tierre asked.

She didn't answer.

"Mum?"

"Sorry, yes, just give me a bit of time. I need to shower first."

In the bathroom she thought about the distress and confusion of the birds as they searched for their young and their home. Her tears mixed with water.

6

Ash was scrolling through social media when her attention was caught by the image of a man in front of the Houses of Parliament. He was holding a sign which read, 'Scientist on Hunger Strike.' Something about his face was familiar. She looked at the name – Professor Michael Lester – and realised it was her tutor from her first two years at university. She read the caption. *Professor Lester has been on hunger strike for four days – he says he will continue until the Government stop investing in new fossil fuel projects.*

She remembered him as an unassuming man, who appeared in no way radical and she was shocked to find him doing something so drastic. Hunger strikes were an extreme form of protest, an almost violent use of the human body, reflecting the violence of the state, employed by people fighting oppression – the Suffragettes, Gandhi, the more recent Irish Hunger Strikes, which happened in her lifetime.

It had been twenty years since she'd last seen him. He must be in his late fifties or sixties by now. She showed the image to Jay.

"That takes courage," he said.

She thought about their petition and their letters and emails which were mostly being ignored.

"I should go to London to see him. He supported me after Mum died. I was in such a state and the college expected me to keep working as if nothing had happened. He noticed I was struggling and let me have extended deadlines for essays. Once we had a long talk about death. Most people avoided the subject, but his first wife died soon after they married – he knew about grief."

*

It was hot. Temperatures were creeping up. Around the world records were being broken. The south of England reached 35 degrees centigrade. A heatwave was officially declared. Water butts dried up. The pond on the reserve shrank and developed large cracks at the edges. The heat was good for the dragonflies that were emerging, hovering over the water, before dipping down to lay their eggs. There were wildfires in Greater Manchester, the largest at Saddleworth Moor, which destroyed trees, nesting sites and vegetation.

The space where the hedgerow had been made her catch her breath whenever she saw it.

*

Michael Lester had been on hunger strike for two weeks – in each new video he seemed to disappear more.

The pavements on Victoria Street radiated heat, the

buildings seemed to be pushing in, suffocating her. She crossed Parliament Square and saw him sitting on the pavement outside the Houses of Parliament, under a large umbrella. There were two men talking to him. She waited until they'd gone then approached.

"Hello, Mr Lester."

He looked up and after a few seconds she could see recognition in his eyes.

"Ash Morton? Is that you?"

"Yes, it's me."

"Well, that's a surprise. What brings you here?"

"I saw your posts. I wanted to come and support you."

"Thank you. It's been a long time."

"Almost twenty years. How are you? I mean, maybe that's a stupid question…"

"I'm doing well; so far."

"This is huge, what you're doing, what made you decide?"

"Well … I'm a scientist and I can see the way things are going. We're burning way too much fossil fuel; we need to get our emissions down."

"What do your family think?"

"My second wife divorced me and moved to Australia. My son won't speak to me until I call this off. My daughter is more understanding. I've told them the seriousness of the situation we're in. People need to stand up and be counted, or in my case sit down." He laughed.

She sat on the pavement next to him. Tourists walking past glanced at them; a child came closer to look at the sign, before being pulled away by the adult with her.

"Some people stop to talk but the majority walk by, they seem embarrassed, but maybe they're just scared."

"They could be, not eating is a dramatic form of protest."

"Yes, I suppose so. I'd like to know about you; how's your life been?"

She told him about Tierre and her work at the reserve.

"I love it. I'm outside all day and I get to inspire young people to fall in love with nature."

He smiled. "You'd be good at that, I remember your passion, especially for bats."

"I've still got that. We have a fight where I live. They want to build a bypass which will destroy an ancient tree called the Whispering Oak and dissect the village. I'm scared for the wildlife, particularly the bats."

He sighed. "Sorry to hear that. How old is the oak?"

"Five hundred years but they deny it. We've started a campaign."

"If anyone can win, you can."

"Do you think the PM will do as you ask?"

He shrugged. "I don't know. There are two MPs who are trying to persuade him, but he seems addicted to fossil fuels."

"I wish I could do something to help."

"You're here. That helps. And keep fighting, fight for that tree with everything you've got."

Tears pricked her eyes and she blinked them away.

"How do you pass the time?"

"When it's quiet I close my eyes and imagine a better world – where no one is dying of heat or in floods. People and wildlife are thriving, the skies are teeming with birds, the air is full of song."

"It sounds wonderful."

The sun glared off the pavement, the heat was burning through the soles of her sandals. She sighed deeply.

"Don't despair, we can still change things," he said.

"Will you… keep going?"

"I think so, though I hope I don't need to of course. I love life. I love my children."

"I wouldn't have the courage to do what you're doing."

He put his hand on her shoulder. "You don't have to. You have a daughter who needs you. You're teaching a new generation about what's important."

She noticed a young man hovering nearby, looking as if he was waiting to say something.

"I should go."

They held hands for a moment; his was cool and she felt the bones under the skin.

"Goodbye Ash and thanks for coming; good luck with your fight."

She walked up Whitehall to Trafalgar Square. She was hungry and, with a feeling of guilt, went to a café and ate falafels with hummus and salad. The waitress asked if she'd enjoyed her meal and she said it was delicious.

*

Sheila and Geoff Duffy led the local bat group and ran the rescue centre. They'd worked with bats for over forty years and were committed to rehabilitating as many sick and injured ones as possible. Their garage had been adapted into a space to care for them and was filled with cages and feeding stations. Sheila was a small, determined woman, with huge amounts of energy.

Ash had gone to see her to talk about the bypass campaign.

"Can we do our own survey of the area around the wood? The Roads Agency may not be as thorough as we need them to be."

"Yes of course. We can do something this weekend, I'll get the group together. Do you want to help me feed this pip? She was hit by a car; the driver liked bats and brought her in. She was underweight, but she's picking up now," Sheila said.

"I'd love to."

Sheila unlocked the cage and, with gloves on, gently picked up the tiny bat.

"The mealworms are in that box."

Ash grasped one of the wriggling creatures and gave it to the bat. She took it in her teeth and began to eat.

Ash laughed. "She's hungry."

"They love to eat. She should be ready for release in a few days."

*

On a clear night eight members of the bat group met at the moon pond. They spread out in pairs, some into the wood and some to the field. Ash was with Sheila and they moved across the common towards Pear Tree Farm, recording Pipistrelles, Daubenton's, Brown Long-Eared bats and a Barbastelle, which was quite rare but had been recorded there before.

The farm was surrounded by a high flint wall, which was collapsing in places. By the wall was a large, semi-derelict barn. They positioned themselves on different sides of the building. Ash waited. The light faded and a waning moon was rising. A star appeared. There was a slight breeze, like a breath, ruffling the back of her hair.

Her phone lit up; the detector emitted a high-pitched, continuous warble which was unfamiliar. A name flashed up: Greater Horseshoe Bat. She studied the screen, amazed, thinking that the detector had got it wrong. She waited, not moving, barely breathing. A shape whipped across her vision, the detector recorded the same sound and ID.

She moved quietly round the corner to find Sheila.

"Listen to this."

She played the recording.

"Woah! That's incredible. A Greater Horseshoe. We've never recorded one in Sussex. Amazing. Let me try with mine."

On the other side of the barn Sheila's detector came to life.

"It really is one. Maybe they're using the barn as a roost. We need to find out."

They waited a while longer but although they picked up other sounds they didn't hear the Greater Horseshoe again. Back at the meeting point Ash told them what she'd found.

"Wonderful news, I'm sorry I missed it," Geoff said.

"Greater Horseshoes haven't been found in Sussex for over two hundred years. It's very exciting, but we need to keep this quiet for the moment to protect them. I'll notify the surveyor immediately and see if she can gain access to the barn," Sheila said.

Ash said, "It might be hard, especially if the Fullers think it might affect the sale."

"We'll try," Sheila said.

When Ash got home, she told Jay about the find but swore him to secrecy.

"OK, I'll keep quiet, but it's good news, right?"

"It's the best. We better not tell Tierre just yet; she probably won't be interested anyway but just in case. It's got to be kept quiet."

7

Sheila called to say that the Fullers had refused to let the bat surveyor access the barn.

"What can we do?"

"The surveyor will try again and then probably make an unannounced visit to see if that works. We may need to be patient."

There was no time for patience – they needed evidence and they needed it soon.

Ash was walking home from work through the wood when she heard someone say hello. She looked around and saw a pair of legs dangling from a branch in a nearby beech tree. She walked over and looked up. A face peered down at her.

"Hi Gavin, what are you doing up there?"

"I like it. Have you got anything to eat?"

"I might have some chocolate." She looked in her bag. "It's 90% cocoa though, not sweet."

"That's OK."

He swung his legs over the branch then hanging by his hands dropped down, as if it was the easiest thing in the world. He ate what was left of the chocolate.

"Are your parents still selling the farm?"

"Yeah. They want the money."

"Where will you go?"

"Dunno. I want to stay. I like the trees. I know what they are, even in winter when there's no leaves, I can tell by the bark."

"Brilliant. Do you know what sort of bats you see at the farm?"

"No but they live in the barn. You can look if you want. I know where the key is."

"I'll have to ask your parents."

"They won't let you."

"Oh, well then I won't be able to."

"They're out on Saturdays. You could come then."

"Are they?" She paused. "I'll have to think about it."

"They won't know."

"Maybe."

"Thanks for the chocolate."

She hesitated then said, "What time's best?"

"They always go at 10am, come after that."

He turned and jumped, caught the first branch and then pulled himself back up into the tree.

*

Over the next two days she thought about Gavin's offer. He was a year ahead of Tierre at school, so he was maybe thirteen or fourteen. She didn't know if she should go into the house without an invite from his parents but… time was running out – the report from the Roads Agency stated there were no rare species of bats in the area. If they didn't establish that the barn was a Greater Horseshoe roost, then it could be destroyed.

On Saturday morning, just after 10am, she went to the farm. There was no sign of the Land Rover. She knocked and Gavin answered the door.

"Alright."

"Hi Gavin."

"Come in."

The hallway was gloomy and the wallpaper was peeling off. Gavin took a key from a hook behind the back door. In the farmyard were several buildings. The barn was at the far end. Some of the timbers in the large wooden door were rotting. Gavin undid the padlock and they went inside.

Her eyes grew accustomed to the dark and she could make out huge wooden beams around the edges of the ceiling. She turned on the infrared torch and shone it along the top of the walls, trying to find something that looked like a bat, but could see nothing there. On the far side was a small door.

She whispered, "Let's look in there. Careful though."

They headed to the corner, stepping over old tyres and skirting round rusting pieces of farm machinery. She pushed open the door. The space inside was almost pitch black, just a sliver of light under the roof, a crack where bats might enter. The beam picked out small shapes in a corner. She moved closer, motioning to Gavin to follow. She could see an upside-down face – a nose the shape of a horseshoe, a body the size of a small pear. There were others clustered together along the beam; as they watched, some of the shapes quivered.

"Wow," Gavin whispered.

She counted at least twenty individuals; wished she had an infrared camera to record the find. After fixing the image in her mind she motioned to Gavin that they should leave, aware that the bats were easily disturbed.

Outside he said, "I told you they were there."

"These bats are special, so we need to keep the roost secret, can you do that?"

"Of course. I don't talk to Mum and Dad and my friends aren't interested in stuff like that."

She'd never seen him with any friends but maybe he had some at school.

"Thanks Gavin. It's great to have seen them."

He smiled and ducked his head, as if unused to anyone saying anything nice to him.

Later she called Sheila.

"That is wonderful news. I'll let the surveyor know, we must record them."

8

Every day the sky was a beautiful blue. She missed the rain – the sound of drumming on the roof, the smell when the first drops hit the dry pavement – the trees and plants reviving as they took in the life-giving water.

Hay fields turned brown. Cows huddled under the trees, desperate for shade, as if they were in Africa. Birds scrabbled in dusty earth looking for scarce grubs. She filled up the bird bath twice a day; everything from the tiniest wren to a crow came to drink and bathe.

A siren clanged through her sleep, waking her with a jolt. Her phone registered 4.45am. It was getting light. She got out of bed and drew aside the curtain. In the distance was a pall of smoke.

Jay turned and muttered, "What's up?"

"Something's on fire, I'm going to look."

She pulled on a t-shirt and shorts, grabbed her keys and jogged down the lane. Further along the road, past the Fullers' place, she could see smoke and flames; a wheat field was burning. She reached the field and could see a fire engine spraying plumes of water onto the flames.

After a few minutes Jay joined her. "That looks bad."

They stood watching. Smoke billowed over the field.

"I hope it won't reach the farm," she said.

Another siren sounded and a second engine arrived, turned into the gate and bumped across the field. A gust of wind blew smoke over them. It was thick and choking, filling her nostrils, making her eyes sting.

"We should go back," Jay said.

They ran up the lane. Ash stopped at the farm, banged on the door and called, "Hello, is anyone there?" There was no answer. "They must be out." She was holding her breath, trying not to inhale too much smoke.

Back in the house, Tierre appeared at the top of the stairs, rubbing her eyes. "What's happening?"

"A wheat field caught fire."

"Is it close to the farm? Is Gavin OK?"

"They're not at home. Two fire engines are there – it looks like the firefighters have it under control," Ash said.

They watched from the upstairs window and gradually the smoke began to disperse.

Later Ash went back to the scene. A large swathe of wheat had been blackened and destroyed and was, in places, still smoking. There was a smell of burnt soil. One of the fire engines was still there, so she went to ask a firefighter if they knew how it had started. He said they didn't know yet; the caller had been anonymous, and asked if she'd seen anything unusual.

"I was sleeping and the siren woke me…" then she remembered something, "…there was a dark grey van parked here yesterday evening, it was blocking the gate to the field. I thought it was odd. I glanced at the licence plate, I think it began with RS, but I don't really remember, sorry."

"That's OK, could be useful."

Jay was pumping up Tierre's bicycle tyres. Ash leant against the shed door. "What if it wasn't an accident? Maybe Andrew Fuller started the fire deliberately? If he found out there are bats in the barn it would make selling the house difficult."

"Isn't that a bit paranoid?"

"The timing's weird though – before the surveyor gained access to the barn?"

He screwed up his face. "Maybe, but remember we're in a drought, there are fires all over the place."

It was true. Wildfires were burning around the country, sometimes started by barbecues or even a glass bottle left carelessly at the edge of a dry field. This was how fragile their world had become.

Ash, who had a good memory for numbers, racked her brain but couldn't remember the rest of the licence plate of the grey van – even if she could it wouldn't prove anything.

*

A few days later she met Gavin in the lane, trying to fix the chain on his bike.

"Mum knows you were in the barn. I forgot to put

the key back. I asked her not to tell Dad, but she said she couldn't promise. I hate this thing." He gave the bike a kick.

"Jay's great at fixing them. Let's take it to my house, see if he can mend it."

He went with her, wheeling the bike.

"You weren't at home when the fire started, were you?"

"We went to my auntie's because they said she was ill, but when we got there, she was alright."

"Have any fire investigators been round?"

"There was some bloke here yesterday. They found a barbecue tray in the field."

"It's an odd place for a picnic. Would it help if I explain to your mum about the barn?"

He shook his head. "Don't bother, it'll probably make it worse."

Tierre came to watch as Jay fiddled around with the chain on Gavin's bike.

"Can you fix it?"

"It needs a special tool which I've got, it won't take long."

"You could come with us on our next ride," Tierre said.

Ash was surprised; usually her daughter was reticent with people she didn't know well.

"OK," Gavin said, straight away.

9

Ash put her ear against the trunk of the Whispering Oak and listened; she could hear a sort of humming, a throbbing heartbeat of life running through it.

In First Nations cultures rivers and forests had rights, but here in the UK trees were inanimate objects that could be removed and destroyed whenever they were thought to be in the way.

All living beings were amazing. Trees talked to each other – an octopus had a central brain and one in each arm, tiny birds such as swallows flew thousands of miles back to the same nest site every year. There was no end to the diversity and wonder of nature. When she was a child, the skies had been filled with screaming swifts, there were flocks of curlew flying over the harbour, filling the sky with sounds of longing, but now these birds were disappearing. People who lived in cities might not notice the changes, but she was aware of even minute changes to nature and the loss of these precious sights and sounds tugged at her heart and made her determined to hang on to what was left.

Her goals for the future were different to those she'd had when younger. They were no longer about her career, or travelling the world, or what Tierre might do when she grew up. Now all she wanted to do was to help protect the land and the wild creatures who lived around her. She was starting to see that it meant coming together with people, forging alliances, finding connections and courage.

The woods and the life that was found there were special, the snowdrops pushing through the cold ground, a nightingale singing, the woodpecker raising its chicks in a hole in a dead tree, delicate purple fungi on their fragile stems, the flash of colour of the yellow brain fungus on a dead birch tree. These were treasures. When she was among the trees she was completely connected, another part of the ecosystem.

She looked up. The trunk was thick, and the first few branches were solid and strong. The spaces between them were an integral part of the structure. A thought occurred: it was the perfect place for a treehouse. She could see where it would fit, between the third and fourth branch. She could live in the oak, with others, and save it from the felling machine. It had been done before. She could sleep closer to the stars and the birds and the bats. It was possible. She was fit enough, she didn't mind heights, loved camping.

The vision, and her courage, soon faded. She was a parent, she loved her hot showers, comfortable bed, coffee in the morning. Living in trees was something other people did, those that were braver and more determined than her.

She leant her head against the trunk, shut her eyes, felt the dappled sun on her face, imagined losing the tree, which had taken hundreds of years to grow and would take only take a few minutes to fell – the stump left behind; the growth rings a testament of a long life, as well as an accusation. The thought broke her heart.

*

The idea of a treehouse went round in her head at work and at night when she was trying to sleep. It needed to be solid enough to support at least two people – others could camp at the base. Beccy might help and maybe Dora. She didn't know about Hazel.

Tierre was nearly thirteen and becoming more independent. She was happy enough at school – had a small circle of friends and was close to Jay. It could work out.

Ash called a meeting. Some of the original members of the action group had drifted away, believing they'd already lost the fight. Six people came.

She said, "I had an email to say that the petition has been rejected. Not enough local people have signed. Most councillors are ignoring my emails."

Beccy said, "Netherley told me that all our concerns had been addressed and there's no more to be discussed."

"The Roads Agency think all the wildlife can be relocated. Mrs Burnett has accepted compensation and agreed to move, so we're not getting anywhere," Liz said, flicking her long hair away from her face with an angry gesture.

"Mum's talking about moving again. Holly has just

settled in at school, it's a nightmare," Dora said.

Ash said, "We could lose access to the wood soon. We need to do something."

"We've run out of ideas," Mark said.

"The only way is to physically block construction. I think we should start a camp at the Whispering Oak," Ash said.

There was silence. Ash looked at their expressions, which were a mixture of surprise and reluctance; then Beccy said, "Are there enough of us?"

"I'll do it; if others can too, we can build a treehouse," Ash said.

"It's a good idea, but my back is messed up. I couldn't climb or camp out. I can make food though," Liz said.

Beccy said, "Trouble is Mum can't do without me. My sister is in Australia so it's just me looking after her. I can support you in other ways."

Mark said, "Sorry, count me out. Sarah would go mad if I tried anything like that."

Ash looked at the other two.

Dora said, "I agree, Ash, it's the only thing left to try. I've finished college for the summer so I can be there."

Hazel said, "It's a good idea, but I need permission from the bishop. Let me see what I can do."

"We can't do it with just two of us," Ash said, disappointed at their reluctance.

"Joanna will be back in a couple of weeks; I'm sure she'll join us," Hazel said.

Liz said, "We can ask around, see if anyone else is

willing to help."

The atmosphere was subdued and after trying to think of other ideas and failing they agreed to end the meeting.

Dora waited while Ash unlocked her bike. "Do you fancy going for a coffee and a chat?"

"That would be great."

They walked into town and chose a small half empty café, ordered coffee and sat at a table in the corner.

Dora said, "I've had an idea. My brother Fly might help. He was at an HS2 camp last year – he's good at protest."

"Do you think he would?"

"Last time we talked he was in Scotland, but I think he's back now. I'll call him."

She punched numbers in her phone and Ash heard an answerphone pick up.

"It's me. Can you call me back?" Dora said, then to Ash, "Have you ever done anything like this before?"

Ash shook her head. "I'm not an activist, I've always focussed on my work, then I had Tierre. I've been on a few marches but that's easy. This feels scary."

She fiddled with her cup, not at all certain she wanted to go ahead with the idea.

Dora was looking at her with a solemn expression. "For my generation everything is frightening, it's like someone threw all the balls up in the air and we don't know how they'll fall. All the things my parents had, you know, a job, a house, those things are not going to happen for many of us. We don't know how the future's going to turn out. People are already dying from what's happening with the climate."

Ash listened, knowing she'd contributed to the crisis. Flights abroad, holidays in Italy and Greece. Now southern Europe was too hot in the summer, heatwaves and wildfires – one destroying a National Park that she'd been to in her twenties.

Dora's phone rang. She said, "Hi. Listen, I'm with my friend, Ash, we're trying to stop a bypass – we need some help to build a camp." The voice on the other end of the phone said something. She replied, "It's in Finsted Woods, they're under threat. Yes, it's happening now. Can you? OK, that's great."

She cut the call. "He says he'll help."

"That's amazing," part of her wishing he'd said no so she wouldn't have to go through with it. "I reckon if there's four of us, we can do it."

"Do you know who owns the wood?"

"Oliver Harrison. He lives on the far side of the village in a house called Meadow Lodge. The family have been there for generations, but I think he's the only one left. A few years ago, I found his Labrador off its lead in the woods and took it back to the house. He was grateful, even offered me a reward. I could try talking to him."

"Good idea. Have you told Jay and Tierre yet?"

"No, I thought I'd wait to see if anyone else would do it before I said anything, now I need to tell them. I hope they'll be OK about it."

"Oh, well good luck."

*

That night, after Tierre had gone to bed, she told Jay she needed to talk.

"I'm listening."

"You know I love you?"

"Yeah – are you going to tell me you're having an affair?" He was trying to be funny, but she didn't laugh.

"No – but I might not be here for a bit."

"Why, where are you going?"

"We're thinking of building a camp at the Whispering Oak – to stop the road."

He looked at her with an expression of disbelief.

"A camp?"

"It's the only way left to stop it. Dora and her brother are going to help and Hazel too, if she gets permission."

"What about Tierre? And work?"

"You're here and I'm owed some time off."

"Do I have a say in it?" He shut his laptop with a snap.

"Of course."

"You sound like you've made up your mind."

Through the window she could see stars and a moon; it seemed wrong to be arguing.

"I have to save the tree."

"You're being selfish. Tierre needs you."

"She needs to see me fight as well."

She remembered her parents arguing over Greenham and Dad calling Mum *selfish*.

"You're obsessed, you can't give up your life for a tree."

"But it's not just the tree, is it? It's everything, we

have to say that's enough, you can't take any more nature – we need it."

"Look, I know how much it means to you but surely we should mean more?" He stood up, his expression furious. "You're on your own with this, I don't agree with it. I'm going out."

He grabbed his phone and jacket.

"Jay, can we...?" But he'd gone.

When they argued he often went for a walk. Usually, he wouldn't be gone long and then they'd talk but this time he was out for a while, so she went to bed. She lay awake wondering if he was right, and she was too obsessed with saving the tree. When he joined her, he turned away, his back a barrier. She tried putting her arm around him, but he moved it away.

When she woke, after a disturbed night, he was already up. She found him in the kitchen.

He said, "You'll have to be the one to tell Tierre."

*

Tierre was lying on the lawn with a book.

Ash said, "I want to talk to you about something important, OK?"

Tierre shut the book and sat up.

"Have I done something?"

"No, why would you think that?"

"It's just that... What is it, then?" She looked worried.

"You know we're trying to protect the oak?"

Tierre nodded.

"We've tried lots of things and they haven't worked."

"I know Mum."

"We've got a new idea. We're going to build a camp in the tree to save it and that means I'll be living there for a while."

Tierre looked at her, checking to see if she was joking. "But you live here."

"It's only for a short time but it means I won't be here at night or when you get back from school. I'm sorry." It was difficult to get the words out.

"I don't want you not to be here."

"I know sweetheart, but I have to fight for the tree."

"What about me?" She looked as if she might cry.

"I'd much prefer to be here, but I think I have to do this."

"It's a stupid road, for stupid cars, why can't they see that? Everyone should ride bikes."

"You're right."

"I hate them." Tierre pulled up a handful grass and tore it into pieces.

"I promise to come back every few days – it may not be for long."

Tierre stood up, her face pale. "Why is that tree more important than me?" Then she ran inside.

Ash followed her upstairs; found her curled up on the bed, shaking with sobs. Ash lay with her and held her.

"I'm so sorry. I promise I'll call you every night and come back when I can, I won't be far away. Your dad will be here."

Tierre cried harder. Ash reassured her that she loved her, at the same time thinking of her own mum being away, it had felt like a long time but might not have been — the house seeming big and lonely without her.

After a while Tierre stopped crying and said, "Where will you sleep?"

"We'll build a treehouse. You could help us design it."

Tierre shook her head. "When will you be back?"

"As soon as I can. You're the most important thing to me, but the tree is a symbol of what we're doing to nature — if I can save it I must. We'll still go on holiday, I promise."

After supper Tierre was quiet, reading and when she went to bed, she said, "You'll still be here in the morning, won't you?"

"Of course."

10

Ash arrived at Meadow Lodge, a large Georgian house, as a young woman was coming out of the door.

"Hi, I'm Ash. Is Mr Harrison in?"

"I'm Sylvia, his granddaughter. He's not well right now, I'm not sure he can see anyone."

"I won't stay long. It's about the bypass."

"Oh – in that case… I'll see what he says."

She went in and Ash could hear voices. When she came out, she said, "You can go in, but don't stay long, he gets tired easily."

He was sitting in an armchair by open double doors, which looked out onto a garden. There was a large pond, almost a lake, full of water lilies. A black Labrador, the one she'd found in the woods, was lying at his feet. It got up and came towards her, wagging its tail. She stroked it.

"Hello Mr Harrison, I'm Ash."

"I remember. You found Bella in the woods. What can I do for you?"

"I'm part of a group who are trying to stop the

bypass. Are you happy with what's happening to your wood?"

"Of course not!" He banged the arm of the chair with his fist. Bella looked up at him and he patted her head. "Sorry. Who would put a road through a place of such beauty? I've lived here all my life. The family have been here for three centuries."

She'd heard the stories. An uncle in the brigades in the Spanish Civil War; his father, Michael Harrison, shot down in WW2 dogfight, bailing out over the Downs, surviving, just. His mother, Agatha, rumoured to have had an affair with a poet, an illegitimate child…

"I'm old now and what I need to do is sit in the garden, watch and listen. So much wildlife. That will be lost. Whatever fence they build around the road the sound will carry. It will be the end of times, the end of my time, which is coming soon enough." He gave a deep sigh. He was thin, the clothes he was wearing too big, as if he was shrinking beneath them. She was reminded of Michael Lester. "My hearing isn't good, but I still know the birds. There's a pair of robins who nest every year, blackbirds, a wren, dunnocks and long tailed tits. A symphony in Spring, it's marvellous." His eyes lit up for a moment, then his shoulders slumped. "I want to fight – my lawyer says we have a good case, but I'm tired, very tired. I don't have the energy for it."

"I'm so sorry. Do you still own the land?"

"For now, but it's being compulsorily purchased, it will go to the Roads Agency at the end of the month."

"I love the wood too, I have a connection to the Whispering Oak, I couldn't bear it if it was cut down."

"It's a magnificent tree – a sapling at the time of the Civil War. There was battle near here, it's extraordinary to think it was a witness to those times."

"We're planning to set up a camp in the wood, is that OK?"

He looked at her, as if summing up her ability to fight, then nodded. "Who's we?"

"Just a group of local people who want to stop the road. There's not many of us."

"If you're doing it to protect the trees then yes." He coughed, a deep catarrhal noise, then grimaced, as if the effort was too much for him. "Please don't say I gave you permission. That could jeopardise any case I might have against them in the future."

"I understand."

"Well, good luck, I hope I'll be here to see it stopped but…" He shrugged.

"Thanks so much."

She let herself out and walked home across the common, stopping to gaze at five swifts screaming overhead, wondering how much time he had left.

*

Ash asked Ella if she could take two weeks off work. Ella said it was a difficult time but as she sympathised with the cause, she'd allow it. The leave would have to be unpaid.

The Stop the Bypass group arranged to meet to begin building the camp. Fly said he'd bring a mate to help and enough wood to make the platform.

Jay was washing up and Tierre was at the kitchen

table doing art homework. There was still tension between her and Jay, although they'd tried to cover it up for Tierre's sake, but now she needed to let them know it was really happening.

Adopting as light a tone as she could manage, she said, "Will you help us to build the camp on Saturday? It would be great if you were both there."

"Sorry, we're taking the bikes to the Downs for a ride. That's what you wanted, wasn't it Tierre?" Jay said.

Tierre looked up at them, then nodded, with an expression that said she knew she'd taken sides.

"Sorry, Mum."

"Oh, OK then. You can come and see it when it's finished."

She went into the living room, swallowing her disappointment. Although she didn't know for certain, she thought Jay might have planned their cycle trip on purpose. His lack of support was hard. Their relationship, apart from a few disagreements about the house – he was tidier than she – was usually harmonious.

She spent the evening in the garden, pulling up some bindweed that had taken a hold, and then went to bed early.

*

On Saturday Ash met Dora, Liz and Hazel at the oak. Soon after, Fly and his friend, Liam, arrived.

Fly looked like Dora, he was tall, his hair was orange, long and wavy, but it was as if someone had decided to smudge the facial features. The nose wasn't as straight, the mouth slightly lopsided. Liam was older, looked strong and wiry.

Introductions over, they stood back and surveyed the oak.

"Yeah, beautiful tree, it needs saving," Liam said. He pointed up. "Those two branches, about twenty foot up, the third and fourth are perfect. We'll use some thick lengths of wood, with slats going across to hold the base – then brace it with rubber straps. You need to learn to climb."

"I've got ropes and harness here," Fly said. "Once we've finished building the structure I'll show you what to do."

They collected wood and tools from the van. Liam climbed the oak and attached a rope ladder for them to use. He measured the space and told them what length to cut. They took turns with the saw. Soon the structure began to emerge. Once he'd attached the slats, they stopped for a break.

"It's solid. When it's complete we can attach a tarpaulin over a higher branch, so you'll keep dry."

Her idea was becoming reality. Ash hoped she'd have the courage to stay and fight.

When it was finished Ash and Dora climbed the ladder and stood on the platform, which was big enough for two people to sleep side by side.

Dora did a tentative stamp with her foot on the base. "It feels strong."

Ash looked over the edge. "It's high enough to make it hard for others to reach us which is great."

Fly had rigged up a hammock in the sister oak. "I

love this," he called.

Back on the ground they started the climbing lesson.

"The rope ladder is fine sometimes but to be able to act quickly and to go higher you need to use a rope. Have you done this before?"

They all shook their heads.

"OK, I'll demonstrate. First thing: this is the harness." He held it up, then climbed into it. "Now attach these metal clips, carabiners. This is the Prusik loop. We need to learn how to make a throwing bundle with the rope, like this." He looped lengths of rope and tied them loosely. "Now attach it to the harness, got that?"

"When you're ready, throw the rope over the branch. Use the second branch, so you have something to stand on." With a deft movement he threw the rope up and over the lowest branch. There was a murmur of assent. "Now, put your feet against the trunk, then pull yourself up, like this." He demonstrated, hauling himself up and onto the first branch, making it look easy.

Letting himself down again, he said, "Who's first?"

Hazel said she preferred to stay on the ground.

Dora said she'd go first. She climbed into the harness and did as he'd showed them with the clips. He checked to make sure they were properly attached.

"OK, you're safe. Right, now have a go with the rope."

She took a throw but missed the branch; tried again and this time the rope went over. "Now put your feet on the trunk." After some fumbling, and going slowly, she managed to raise herself up onto the first branch.

"Well done, sis."

Ash was next. Conscious of being watched, she made two failed attempts at the throwing.

"Take your time," Fly said.

Next throw worked and following what she'd been shown she pulled herself up, managing to get a foothold on the lower branch, and held onto the one above.

"Great, do as I showed you and let yourself down."

Her feet touched the ground. "Made it!"

They practised a couple more times, then Fly said, "OK, that's enough for now. You've both got the idea. We'll be getting back."

"Good luck, I can come down again if you need another body," Liam said. "Just one warning – try to avoid the national bailiffs. They're the ones that dragged us out at Brooke Wood. They're violent, nearly broke my arm. We had lights shone on us at night, machinery being used all hours. Friends brought food and water but were stopped from giving it to us."

"That makes me feel better," Ash said.

"Sorry, don't mean to scare you. There are good things too. One, you know you're on the right side of history, two you get to hang out with some great people, three, you get to shit in the woods," Liam said. They laughed.

"We need to be ready to move into the camp as soon as work starts. It could be as early as next week," Ash said.

"I'm free so that's not a problem," Dora said.

"I'm still waiting for the bishop to give permission. I'll send him a reminder tonight," Hazel said.

"We need to think about food and a support network. Beccy said she'll do social media and respond if there's any press interest," Ash said.

"I'll bring hot food in the evening as often as I can," Hazel said.

*

It was Ash's last weekend at home, she didn't know for how long. On Sunday they went to the beach. The water was a shimmering azure blue, a heat haze hung over the horizon and there was no breeze. They swam and played in the waves, and no one mentioned what was happening next week.

Tierre and Jay constructed a dolphin out of sand, they played frisbee and Tierre did handstands, perfectly balanced for a second or two, silhouetted against the sea and cloudless sky. The day stretched out.

Then it was time to leave.

"We need to go, love, it's getting late," Ash said, but Tierre sat with her knees drawn up, chin resting on them and didn't move.

"What if we never come back?"

"We will, I promise."

"But you're going to live in a tree."

"It's not forever."

Jay was packing things away and didn't say anything.

"We can have pizzas and watch a movie – anything you like." Desperate to make herself and her daughter feel better.

Watching the film, Ash took Tierre's hand. It felt small. She already missed her.

When she and Jay were in bed she said, "I'm sorry."

"I know."

He turned to look at her – no longer angry. She moved close and put her arm around him.

*

Ash kept a close watch on the construction site. On Tuesday morning a lorry arrived with piles of fencing on the back.

She rushed out a message, "Get here as soon as you can." Replies from Dora and Fly. "There by 5pm."

Jay was at work and Tierre at school. Ash began packing. Changes of underwear and t-shirts, a spare pair of jeans, toothbrush and toothpaste. She hesitated over the soap; washing would be difficult. Food was apples, nuts, dried fruit, carrots, chocolate. Liz and Hazel would bring hot food. She had a book, a torch, her phone was fully charged.

When she'd finished, she lay on the bed and looked out of the window at the sky, luxuriating in the comfort of the mattress, hoping the plan would work and she'd be home again soon.

Jay returned with Tierre. She met them at the door – he noticed her packed rucksack.

"You're going, then?"

"It's started. Hazel is coming to pick me up soon."

Tierre put down her bag, went into the living room and sat on the sofa. Ash followed her.

"Do you have to go?"

"I'm sorry, sweetheart, I do."

She sat next to her. Tierre was rigid at first, then she leaned in.

"I love you, so much," Ash said.

"I love you too, Mum."

Jay was in the kitchen. She could tell he was upset by the way he held his shoulders.

"I'll be back as soon as I can."

"I hate this, I feel like we're being pulled apart."

"I know but it won't be for long."

She hugged him.

"Be careful."

"I will, I promise."

Hazel rang the bell and Ash picked up her rucksack and went out. Tierre and Jay stood at the top of the steps. Tierre was holding Swimmy to her chest. As Ash got into the car Tierre called, "Swimmy says goodbye," waving its flipper.

As they drove off Hazel said, "Are you OK?"

Ash was swallowing back tears. "That was hard."

"I'm sorry."

Ash blew her nose, trying not to think about Tierre.

Hazel said, "Good news – the bishop said yes to me taking a few days off. I wasn't completely honest with him. I said I was supporting people who want to save an ancient tree. Not that I might stay there too; not very Christian."

"What happens if he finds out?"

She shrugged. "I don't know."

*

Dora and Fly were sitting under the oak. These people, whom she hardly knew, were to be her family for a while. They greeted each other with hugs.

"Fences are up around the south part of the wood, so it looks like they're starting there," Ash said.

"We need to be ready for whatever happens," Fly said.

They set up a place for cooking with a small stove, a container of water and a bowl, hanging a tarpaulin to protect it. There'd been no rain for weeks and none was forecast, so it was mainly a precaution.

Hazel had brought camping stools and some cups and plates. "There's a vegetable stew for tonight."

She set a pan on the stove and when it was hot spooned the food into bowls. They sat down to eat.

Dora said, "Was Tierre OK when you left?"

"I don't know. She wasn't as upset as last week; I hope she'll be alright tonight."

"My friends say I'm crazy. They don't think what's happening to the climate is anything to do with them, it's too far away. They mostly worry about money and their careers. I never imagined doing anything like this. I was always going to be a dancer, but I've been with Holly during an asthma attack and it's terrifying. The last time, she was on a ventilator in hospital."

"That's awful," Ash said.

Fly said, "So many people are killed by air pollution around the world, it's horrific."

"How long were you at Brooke Wood?" Ash asked.
"Two months."

"A long time," Ash said, inwardly wondering what

would happen to them.

"I was scared when you were there, it was violent," said Dora.

"We stuck together, that way we were strong. Even though we lost hundreds of trees, it was good we stayed and witnessed what happened."

The sun was going down.

"I'm off home but I'll come by tomorrow evening with more food. Message me if you need anything before then," Hazel said.

Ash sent a message to Tierre with heart emojis but there was no reply. Standing in the darkening wood, brushing her teeth, was a strange experience.

She climbed the rope ladder to reach the platform. The wood creaked slightly when she stepped onto it but felt solid beneath her feet.

Dora joined her, "This is magical."

There was a full moon rising, a June strawberry moon, and through the canopy of the oak Ash could see the line of the sea.

"I would love being here if I wasn't scared about what might happen."

"Like Fly said, if we stick together, we'll be OK," Dora said.

Ash didn't know if Dora was always that optimistic or whether she was just trying to reassure them.

They laid out their sleeping bags and mats. She put a photo of Tierre under the small cushion she had for a pillow and got into the sleeping bag.

"Is it comfortable?"

"So far."

"That's good, though I can sleep anywhere."

They said goodnight.

There was a slight breeze which rustled the leaves. Rooks chirruped as they settled down in a nearby tree. Ash lay awake. There was snuffling and rustling beneath, maybe a fox out for a night prowl for food. Despite the lack of rain, the wood smelt damp and earthy.

She listened to her heartbeat and the sounds of the night, conscious of being alive and connected to a vast web of life.

11

Ash opened her eyes – sunlight through leaves – remembering she was in the Whispering Oak with Dora. Jay and Tierre were at home, probably still asleep.

Needing to pee she got out of the sleeping bag, unrolled the ladder and climbed down. She went into the wood and squatted behind a tree.

Early morning mist, soon to burn off, hung over the common. The work site was quiet. She filled the kettle with water and lit the stove. A large bumblebee flew past heading for the honeysuckle entwined in a bush nearby. She drank tea and stood watching as the mist began to clear. The boards creaked above and soon Dora joined her.

"Hello."

"Hi. Did you sleep?"

"Really well, I woke up once and wondered where I was, then I went off again." Dora yawned. "Did you?"

"Mm. Off and on. Do you want tea?"

"Herb tea is great."

"I need to get used to doing without coffee," Ash said.

"I never drink caffeine; it makes me shaky."

Fly was singing in the hammock – "It's a beautiful day." He let himself down the rope and joined them, looking cheerful. "Alright rebels?"

There was an engine noise in the lane – they watched the gate at the far side of the field, but nothing appeared. Ash's stomach was tense.

"I'm going to have to keep myself occupied, otherwise I'll get jumpy," she said.

"We could do a dance warm up. I do one most days, I can teach you if you like, it's easy," Dora said.

"Great."

"Right, we start like this." Dora began to do neck stretches and head rolls, then shoulder and arm rolls. "Good, keep going, slow and steady. Now we'll do some jogging on the spot, then some jumping jacks, they're good exercise."

Dora was bouncing up and down and was hardly out of breath. After a while Ash collapsed on the grass, breathing heavily. "That's it, I'm done. God, I'm unfit."

Dora laughed. "You did OK. It's a good work out."

They ate a breakfast of bread and peanut butter, with apples. Ash was enjoying getting to know these siblings, both in their early twenties, who had more awareness and more determination than many of Ash's generation. If she didn't think about what could happen, she might feel almost blissful.

"I brought some paper and coloured pencils, I had an idea that we could write notes for the workers and pin them on the fence, like they did at Greenham Common. We can tell them what will be lost if the road goes ahead," Ash said.

"Good idea, but I'm dyslexic, I'll draw instead," Fly said.

Ash wrote about the bats trying to find their way across the new road, the lights dazzling them, disconnecting them from their hunting routes, and about the oak, the times it had lived through, the people who had sheltered under it, all the storms it had survived.

Fly showed them his drawings. There were animals and birds, the flash of orange of a fox, the distinctive head stripe of a badger, the red, black and white of a woodpecker. They were sketches but he'd captured the essence.

"They're beautiful," Ash said.

Dora had covered several pieces of paper in small writing. "It's about Holly and how the air pollution affects her."

They tied the messages to the fence where the workers would see them.

"Even if one person reads them it could make a difference," Ash said.

Dora and Ash practised climbing. It was getting easier but though she was used to gardening, Ash's hands were soon sore from the hard rope and the rough oak bark.

Morning turned to afternoon. Tierre would be returning from school.

Hazel arrived with a pot of food. "Has anything

happened?"

"Not yet," Ash said.

"Joanna's back from Colombia at the weekend; I'm hoping she'll join us. She's strong, no one can intimidate her."

After eating Ash called Jay. "Hi, it's me, I'm OK, can I talk to Tierre first?"

"Sure."

"Hi Mum." Tierre told her about school and what she and Maya were doing, but after a few minutes she said, "I've got to go, I've got loads of homework, here's Dad."

"Is she OK?"

"She's fine, a bit subdued but that's not surprising."

"Thanks."

"Don't worry, I'm keeping an eye on her." His attempt at reassurance didn't help. "What's happening there?"

"Work hasn't started yet, we're just waiting, it's hard."

He was quiet – she knew he was thinking she should come home.

"Are you OK?"

"I'm fine, well… you know."

He didn't say anything else so she said, "I'll call again tomorrow. Give Tierre a hug from me."

"I will. Take care."

That night the boards felt harder, she shifted about trying to get comfortable. Eventually she slept. When she woke Dora wasn't there.

A shout – "They're here."

She yanked on trousers and went as fast as she dared down the ladder.

Two lorries, with machinery on the back, were bumping across the field and came to a halt near the fence. Workers jumped out of the cabs.

Fly was watching through binoculars. He handed them to her. "Not sure what that is on the back."

"Looks like a JCB and there's something else – hope that's not a tree felling machine." She swallowed, fear in the pit of her stomach.

As she watched one of the workers began to cross the field towards them.

"There's someone coming."

"Do we stay here or go back up?" Dora said.

"He's on his own, let's see what he wants," Ash said.

They stood close together, guarding the tree. The worker was young and looked curious, rather than threatening.

"Did you put the messages on the fence?" he asked.

Ash nodded.

"Are you those eco-people?"

"We're people who love this wood and don't want it to be destroyed," Ash said.

"What's your name?" Dora asked.

"Jamie."

"I'm Dora, why don't you join us?'

He laughed. "Don't think so, I need this job."

"We need nature and wildlife – ecosystems are collapsing everywhere," Fly said.

"Everything looks OK. Sun's out, the birds are singing."

"The thing is, it's too hot, we're in a drought. And there's hardly any insects. We can't survive without insects," Ash said.

He looked blank. "Nobody's going to let it get that bad."

"It's already that bad for some people," Fly said.

"Anyway, I just came to warn you. The boss knows you're here... he's not happy. You should get out while you can."

He walked away.

"I think we should go back up," Ash said.

Soon after, two men arrived. They stood under the Whispering Oak and peered up.

The older one called, "I'm in charge here. I don't know what you're doing but you need to leave before we call the police."

"The wood doesn't belong to you."

"As of yesterday, it does."

Ash looked at Dora, "Maybe they're lying," she mouthed. She called, "That's not what we were told."

"Felling gear will be here soon."

Fly shouted, "We're not going anywhere."

"Tell that to the police."

They walked away, the boss on his phone.

Fly called, "Probably just a threat."

"He didn't seem as if he was messing around," Ash said.

"He was nasty," Dora said.

Ash was unsettled by the encounter – she'd known there'd be confrontation but in her mind had placed it somewhere in the future.

The JCB was digging fifty yards away, pounding, twisting round to dump the mound of soil, then back again for more. They could feel the rumbling through the earth.

They waited, sitting on the edge of the platform; ate nuts and dates to stave off hunger. Ash had her first pee in the bucket. Dora had already peed openly which made her less embarrassed. They passed the time telling stories about their lives; Dora and Fly's childhood in South London; she'd been shy, unlike her brother, then she'd discovered a dance class and found a way to express herself. Ash told her about a trip to a bat cave in Romania, the awe when millions of creatures emerged at dusk. Fly was playing guitar and singing. They kept a look out for signs of police.

Jamie returned in the afternoon. He called, "I read the messages. They got to me, especially the bit about the girl, Holly, but I can't lose my job, my girlfriend is pregnant. I talked to the others, but they just laughed. Felling is due on Monday. It only takes a few minutes to take down a tree, even one this size. I thought you'd want to know."

Dora and Ash's expressions of horror reflected back to each other. Ash imagined watching the tree felling – as she'd done the hedge slaying – this would be worse. They hugged.

"We won't let that happen," Ash said.

After the workers had left for the day, they climbed down from the trees. Hazel arrived and they told her about Monday.

"We need more of us. I'll ask Liam if he can make it," Fly said.

"Joanna will be here by then."

"Six would be good," Ash said.

The rest of the week was the same. Digging continued in the field and the line got closer every day, but the police didn't arrive and the boss kept away.

One morning early, before the workers arrived, Fly went to check the site. When he returned, he said, "There's a grey van parked at the edge of the field. I can't see anyone inside. It's smart, not like a work van, a bit suspicious."

"It could be the same one I saw before the field burned down. I might remember it."

They went to look. The van was dark grey and new.

"It looks the same and the numberplate is familiar, begins with RS like I thought," Ash said.

They peered through the windows but there was nothing on the seats or dashboard to indicate who it belonged to. The back door windows were blacked out.

"Maybe they're spying on us," Ash said.

"Could be. They'll lose money if there's a delay."

They walked back.

"What's it like being arrested?"

"The first time was OK, I wasn't there long. The last time was in January – they took me to a station outside London and kept me for hours, let me out in the middle of the night, it was freezing, I had no money and had to walk ten miles home. That was before the new laws, now it could be worse."

"It sounds awful."

"At least I didn't get put on remand like some of my friends."

*

Beccy sent a message saying that a local journalist wanted to interview them about the camp, so Ash agreed to speak to her. The woman arrived later that day and seemed sympathetic but when the article came out it had misquoted Ash, called them "scruffy eco-protestors" and added a quote from Netherley – the camp was an embarrassment; the majority of law-abiding people wanted the bypass to go ahead.

12

Ash called Tierre.

"Hi Mum, I'm OK. Maya's staying the night and Dad's taking us to the beach on Sunday."

"That sounds nice. Wish I was coming too."

She was relieved that Tierre sounded happy; for a second, thought maybe she wasn't missed, then she was angry with herself for being pathetic.

She told Jay about the grey van.

"I'm sure it's the one I saw near the field. I think we're being watched. Netherley's determined to make sure the bypass goes ahead; it makes you think he's got something invested in it."

"Do you want me to see if I can find anything out?"

"Yes, please… I miss you."

"I miss you too. I feel like a single parent and I'm not very good at it. Sometimes Tierre seems so independent, then other times she's needy; I don't know what to expect."

"I know what it's like to be a teenage girl. Just being there and sounding interested is important, she'll tell you stuff if she wants, but don't push."

"OK, I'll try."

*

Next morning Dora got a phone call. "Hi Mum, how are… what… Is he OK? Oh, yes, we'll come."

She cut the call.

"Dad's in hospital, they think he had a heart attack. We need to be there."

"I'm so sorry, of course, you must go," Ash said.

Dora called for Fly who emerged from the wood, zipping his trousers.

"What's up?"

She told him.

"That sounds bad. We better go, will you be OK, Ash?"

"I'll put out a message for support," Ash said.

Hazel responded straight away, said she was sorry she couldn't make it, she was with a sick parishioner.

No one else replied.

"It's Friday night, they're busy," Ash said.

Dora and Fly were collecting what they needed. "If no one comes you should go home, nothing will happen on Saturday, you shouldn't be here alone. One of us at least can be back tomorrow," Fly said.

"If they're watching they'll know we've left. They might destroy the camp. I want to stay."

"We agreed, no one should be on their own," Dora said.

"Don't worry, look, you go, I'll figure it out."

They hugged her.

After they'd gone Ash had a couple more messages. No one could be there. She thought about going home, cuddling up with Tierre and Jay, having a shower, sleeping in a bed – but the idea of leaving the Whispering Oak unprotected was scary. They might seize the chance to take it down. She couldn't risk it.

She ate a supper of tinned soup, with bread. She thought about calling Jay but if she said she was alone he'd go mad, tell her to come home.

She tidied up then climbed into the tree, pulling the ladder up after her. Although it was strange being there alone, she felt at home. She breathed in the smells of the wood, the earth, the faint scent of honeysuckle, the damp woodiness of the bark. The sounds were familiar, a flutter of leaves, the rustle of a small creature below, a breath on her cheek that she imagined was a bat's wing brushing past.

In the middle of the night, something – a noise or a presence – woke her. She lay still, listening. At first there was silence and she thought she must have been mistaken, then a twig cracked. It might just be the fox on its nightly prowl looking for food, but she was spooked enough to get out of the sleeping bag. She felt for the torch and crawled to the edge of the platform. Peering over she could make out a figure beneath the tree. Adrenaline surged through her. She pointed the torch down and caught a glimpse of someone disappearing into the wood. Thinking it could be the Fuller's boy, she called, "Gavin, is that you?" but there was no reply. She shone the beam round and around, but the person had either gone or was keeping very still.

Her heart was beating fast in her chest. Wanting to sound powerful, she called out, "Go away and leave us alone," in as loud a voice as she could muster but there was no response. She was frightened and grateful for the thirty feet between her and the ground. The rope ladder was up and there was no way anyone could climb the tree unless they had equipment. If they tried, she had a useful weapon, a bucket with pee in it.

She sat tight against the trunk of the oak – wanting to call someone but thinking their phones would be on silent. After a while, her back and legs started going numb. There was no more noise, so whoever it was must have gone. She crawled back into the sleeping bag and fell asleep, just as it was getting light.

It was 7am when she woke, head fuzzy. She sat up, remembering the night visitor. Down below everything looked the same, except the lid of the largest water bottle had come off; it had been tipped over and most of the water had leaked out. She was sure she'd tightened it. Someone must have been there. She sat on a stump, overwhelmed by a sense of isolation and defeat. She was still there when Hazel arrived.

"Are you OK?"

She shook her head.

"What's wrong?"

Ash told her. "It was a bit scary. It might just have been someone curious about the camp but why knock over the water bottle? Unless they wanted to intimidate us." She put her head in her hands. "The worst thing about what happened is that I started doubting everything. I'm away from Tierre, we don't know if what we're doing will work, they can easily evict us."

Hazel put a hand on her shoulder.

"It's OK to have doubts, I have them often, am I better off doing something else, is the Church too oppressive as an institution, even does God really exist. It's hard to see the effect we're having but it may be more powerful than we know. We're trying something, that's important."

Hazel made tea and they ate breakfast.

The daylight and company cheered Ash, and a sense of hope slowly returned.

*

Fly came back on his own; Dora had decided to stay another night.

"Dad's out of intensive care. Sorry you were on your own, Ash."

"I should have just gone home."

"They want to scare us."

"Well, it worked."

They tidied and re-organised the camp, Fly whistling as he worked.

Later Jay called. "I've been researching Netherley's business interests. Seems he's not as squeaky clean as he makes out. For several years he had a second job as a director in a firm of bailiffs. There's a police investigation into some of their methods. In one case bailiffs evicted a disabled man and pulled him out of his wheelchair. He was badly hurt."

She thought about what could have happened in the night and shuddered.

"Is he still involved with the firm?"

"That's proving difficult to find out."

"But the PM's promoting him?"

"Yep."

She sighed.

"Are you OK?"

"I'm just tired. It's hard to keep believing I'm doing the right thing. I miss Tierre, I miss you." She tried to stop herself from crying and failed.

"Come home, Ash."

"I can't – not yet."

There was silence. "I'll come by later with Tierre."

"That would be great."

*

Across the field the workers were edging nearer.

Jay and Tierre arrived. Fly asked Tierre if she wanted to try using the rope. To Ash's surprise she said yes. She seemed fascinated by him; sneaking looks from under her fringe. He showed her how to put on the harness and helped her to go up a little way on the rope.

"This is cool, can I look at the platform now?"

"Let's go up the rope ladder," Ash said.

They climbed up.

Tierre looked around.

"I love it, it's like a secret place."

"You could stay with me tonight if you like, Dora isn't back until tomorrow."

Tierre thought about it for a moment then shook her head. "No, it's OK, Mum, I like being at home."

Ash felt a pang of disappointment but just said,

"Whatever you want sweetheart."

Tierre hugged her. "It's good you're here."

Ash was surprised. "Do you think so?"

She nodded. "Maya's mum showed me the interview you did, she said Netherley was lying and that what you're doing is good – I should be proud of you."

Jay told her that Michael Lester had decided to call off the hunger strike. The Prime Minister had refused to do as he asked but had agreed to a briefing from scientists about the dangers of global warming.

"I hope he didn't risk his health for nothing," Ash said.

13

Dora was back and Joanna arrived from Colombia. She and Hazel pitched a tent behind the oak. They talked and shared their stories, made meals and ate together – in the evening Fly taught them his songs. Ash felt a strong bond growing between them. They were ready for Monday.

Late on Saturday afternoon Sheila called. The surveyor had finally gained access to the Fullers' farm and found a small colony of Greater Horseshoe Bats roosting. They had applied for an injunction to stop the construction work.

There were cheers when she told the others.

"Wow amazing, good for the bats," Dora said.

"It's brilliant news but we don't know if they'll grant one. I want to stay to be sure," Ash said.

"We'll be here too, won't we, Fly?" Dora said.

"Of course."

Joanna said, "I haven't had one night at home for months, which is exactly the way I like it."

*

On Sunday Ash was cutting vegetables for stew when Jay called. "I think you need to come home, something has upset Tierre."

"Is she OK?" Ash had a sudden panic that she should have been there.

"She's fine physically, she won't tell me what it is. I think she needs to talk to you."

"Go be with your daughter," Fly said. "We're fine. I can always ask Liam to come down if we need reinforcements."

"OK but call me if anything happens."

Hazel dropped Ash home. She unlocked the front door and called, "I'm back." No one answered. She found Jay in the shed.

"Hello." She gave him a hug.

"I'm glad you're here. Tierre's in her room. I've asked her what's going on, but she says I won't understand."

"I'll go and see."

She knocked on the bedroom door, said, "It's me, can I come in?" and heard a quiet, "OK."

Tierre was sitting on the bed staring out of the window.

"What's wrong?"

Tierre looked at her but didn't speak.

Ash put her arm around her. "Can you tell me?"

Tierre leant against her. "Maya says she's moving. Her dad wants them to live with him, but she doesn't want to go, she hates him."

"That doesn't sound good."

"She won't be at school anymore."

Grace sometimes found it hard to find enough acting and voiceover work and wondered if a move could be for financial reasons.

"When are they moving?"

"I don't know. I don't want her to go." Tierre was clutching the pillow to her stomach.

"I'll call Grace and see if there's anything we can do to help."

"But what?"

"I don't know yet, let's see what she says. Why didn't you tell your dad?"

"He doesn't understand about people, he only cares about riding his bike and work."

"He cares about you – you know that don't you?"

"Suppose."

"Maybe he doesn't always tell you."

"Are you back now?"

"I can stay tonight and maybe longer. I'll call Grace later. Let's go downstairs. We can make pancakes for supper, if you like."

Grace told Ash that her husband wanted her back and was using his wealth to tempt her.

"I thought about it because we're really struggling but when I asked Maya, she was adamant she didn't want to. She must have got it into her head that I'd agreed but I wouldn't go against what she wants. I'm auditioning next week and I'm hopeful about this one."

"Oh, that's a relief, I'd miss you and Tierre would really miss Maya. I'll tell her, she'll be happy."

That night Ash lay awake thinking she shouldn't have got Tierre's hopes up until they knew something for definite.

Next day Sheila called and told her the injunction had been refused. The judge had ruled that it was safe for the bats to be moved to another roost.

It was like a punch in the stomach.

"I can't believe it. Can we appeal?"

"I'm sorry, Ash. We don't have the funds," Sheila said.

Ash went into the garden. It was almost dusk, a crescent moon was rising, a tiny sliver, crafted from silver, suspended in the sky. It was so exquisite that it almost took her breath away. She wanted to capture the image, hold it and keep it safe, protect it from the endless destruction of the web of life.

*

"When will you be back?"

"I don't know, sweetheart."

"Why does it have to be you?"

Ash sighed. "Because – because I can, I can't explain any more than that, I'm sorry."

Tierre picked at a scab. Ash put a hand gently over her arm.

"Don't hurt yourself. Be angry with me instead."

"You're mean – it's nearly the summer holidays, what will I do if you're still in the tree?"

"I hope it will be over by then. I promise we'll do something nice as soon as I'm back."

*

They were standing on either side of the bed.

"She hates you being away," Jay said.

"You understand though, don't you?"

"If you want the truth, then no. I thought we were the most important things in your life – now I don't know."

"You are – but this is bigger than us; we need to take a stand. We're losing so much."

She wanted to scream at those in power who'd created conflict with her family.

"I have to leave tomorrow, let's not fight, please."

He sat on the bed and muttered something.

She sat next to him. "What?"

"I had a weird dream last night; it was like one I used to get as a kid."

"What about?"

"Mum. She comes to the door and I'm pushing her out. I'm angry, shouting, maybe I shouted in my sleep I don't know. I always told you that when she left I never saw her again. That wasn't true, she did leave but she stayed nearby. She went to live with another man."

"Why didn't you tell me?"

"I don't know I think I was ashamed." He put his head in his hands. "It was so confusing. I watched Dad shrivel up; he lost his sense of purpose, humiliated I suppose. I was only ten, Danny was seven, it was hard. We sometimes passed her in the street and she'd try to speak to us, but Danny and me ran away. I always thought it was my fault she'd gone."

"Of course it wasn't."

"She tried to reach out to me a year ago, I think

Auntie Jean must have given her my email address. She said she was sorry for what she did, but I never replied."

"Maybe you should."

"I don't know."

"I'm not her."

She put her arms round him and he didn't pull away.

14

The alarm went off at 6am. She kissed Jay. "Sorry, I have to get up, the workers might come early."

She hugged Tierre, holding her close to remember the feel of her. They dropped her off at the field.

"Stay safe," Jay said.

"I will."

Dora, Fly, Liam, Hazel and Joanna were there and soon after Mark arrived.

"This is a surprise," Ash said.

"I thought I better to do something. I've brought a tent and can stay a couple of nights. Sarah's not happy but I told her I needed to be here. Sorry I haven't been much help before. I hoped the petition and emails would work."

"It's good you're here now."

"My son said, 'Dad, you have to fight for my future, that's your job, right?'"

She laughed. "Blunt but true."

They gathered in a circle to discuss what might happen.

"Remember – say as little as possible. If the police arrive, they'll be looking for grounds to arrest you. Don't talk to them, they may ask questions, but you don't have to answer. And if they ask, no one is in charge," Liam said.

"We'll stick together on the ground," Hazel said. "They won't want to deal with a vicar."

"Depends on the police, some of them don't care who they arrest, you could be ninety-nine years old," Fly said.

"They won't get us out of the trees easily, so whatever happens we can delay them," Dora said.

They moved close and put their arms around each other, like footballers before a penalty shoot-out.

An engine noise pierced the quiet. Two lorries, one with a trailer carrying a large ugly machine, black with yellow stripes, and the other a cherry picker, appeared at the edge of the field, followed by two police cars and a van.

"They're here. Let's get in position. Good luck," Ash said.

They scrambled up into the trees and Mark, Hazel and Joanna positioned themselves at the base.

Dora and Ash attached their ropes to branches above the platform and sat at the edge so they could see what was happening. The police cars and van appeared below. Uniformed officers emerged and stood in a circle around the tree. Ash glimpsed two men in black standing at the back.

One of the officers spoke into a loudhailer.

"We have an eviction notice. You must now leave

the area."

They remained silent. The three under the tree were holding hands.

"If you don't go now, you'll be arrested."

Still silence.

One of the officers approached Hazel, who was in her vicar's robe.

"Vicar, you must lead by example. Surely you don't want to be involved in criminal activity?"

"God is nature. To fell a healthy tree is a crime."

"Not in this case."

"I disagree."

"We'll give you ten minutes to change your mind."

"We won't."

Dora whispered to Ash, "Do you think they mean it?"

"We'll soon find out."

A voice in the loudhailer, "You all need to come down or we'll be forced to remove you."

Liam and Fly were singing, "We need our trees, we won't let you hurt them, we love our trees, we don't desert them."

Half an hour passed – officers again approached those on the ground and repeated the arrest warning. No one moved.

They arrested Hazel first. Liam had demonstrated how to let their body go floppy as they were picked up and it took four officers to carry her away. Soon they came back for Mark and Joanna.

"I hope Hazel won't lose her job. We're next, are you ready?" Ash said.

"Think so. I won't resist though, I don't want to risk an injury," Dora said.

"Definitely not."

The loudhailer. "Come down now. If you don't, climbers will get you out."

Liam and Fly were still singing.

The cherry picker was manoeuvred close to the base of the sister tree then raised, with a man in climbing gear on the platform. Fly was dangling from a branch. He swung away to escape but the man caught his rope. There were jeers from Liam and sounds of Fly swearing, but they couldn't see exactly what was happening.

Dora was holding onto the railing of the treehouse looking frightened.

Ash put a hand on hers. "He'll be OK."

After a while Fly appeared on the platform with the climber, who signalled for it to be lowered.

When he was on the ground, Fly called up, "I'm fine."

The cherry picker rose again. Liam had climbed to a higher branch and was squatting on it, singing and laughing. He evaded the climber for a while but eventually he was caught and taken to the ground.

"I'm scared," Dora said.

"Me too," Ash said.

An engine started up and then moved away.

"Maybe they've gone," Dora said.

Ash was looking through a gap with the binoculars. "I think that was the van leaving, they must have taken them to the police station."

They waited. Ash's stomach was tense. She drank

water, but not too much; they could be there a long time.

"This is worse, the waiting, not knowing what will happen next. If they take us, that's it for the oak, it will be unprotected. That machine, I'm sure it's for felling, it's not like anything I've seen before."

After two hours nothing had happened. There was no word from Fly or the others so they must still be in the station.

The van returned and the cherry picker was manoeuvred close to the Whispering Oak.

"You go first, I'm staying as long as I can," Ash said.

"Don't put yourself in danger, will you?" Dora said.

The man on the platform appeared close to them. He was unsmiling and had the air of someone who assumed his task would soon be over.

He climbed into the treehouse and said, "Which of you is first?"

Dora nodded and he reached out and took her arm.

"There's no need to force me."

He cut the rope attaching her to the tree, then guided her onto the platform. When they reached the ground, she signalled up to Ash that she was OK and was taken away.

Ash was alone.

She pressed herself against the trunk of the oak, whispered, "One day you'll die, but not yet." Checking that her harness was fitted, she threw the rope over a higher branch, took a deep breath, pulled herself up and sat astride it. Her confidence in climbing had grown – she would go higher if needed.

There was a whirring noise and the cherry picker appeared below. The climber peered through the foliage, taking a moment to spot her.

"You're putting yourself at risk; you need to come down." His tone was reassuring but she wasn't fooled.

Fear hovered but she pushed it to the extremities of her body and found a core of determination there, ready for her. She looked up. The branch above was narrow, but she thought it would hold her weight. After one failed attempt, she managed to throw the rope over and pull herself up.

His voice, more aggressive now, "I will reach you."

Her stomach was in knots. There was a slender branch above. She remembered the strength of oak trees and climbed. Now she was high.

She heard him swearing and waited to see what he would do. He attempted to climb onto the branch that she'd left but his weight made it creak and bow.

"The longer you stay the worse it'll be for you."

Ignoring his threat, she watched to see what he would do next. He must have decided he couldn't get any higher and, after more cursing, he climbed down.

She and the oak were safe, for the moment. The ground, which she could see through a small gap, was at least fifty feet below. Her arms ached from the effort of climbing. She lay along the branch, wound the rope around herself and resolved to stay as long as she could. It was comfortable enough for now.

Her mind wandered – an image of Clara floating in the lemon-yellow dress, her father and brother in mourning below. She imagined hearing voices from the past drifting up to her, travellers in earlier centuries who'd stopped to take shelter from the rain, or the sun, resting and drinking water from a flask, or men and women bringing their pigs to eat the acorns.

Her mind jerked back to the present. Her friends were probably at the station being charged or maybe let go with a warning. She thought of her mum at Greenham Common and wished she'd asked her more about it. Had she been in danger, had she been scared?

Her phone was in a back pocket, so she had no idea of the time. The bark was rough and after a while began to dig into her belly. She shifted and slipped slightly, managing to pull herself back up. Her mouth was dry. It was quiet below as if everyone had left. Maybe it was a tactic to make her feel isolated and vulnerable. She needed to pee and she needed water.

More time passed, she was slightly dizzy from the effort of holding on and the lack of water, but still she wanted to stay. Then there were voices. She couldn't see who it was. Someone called out.

"Ash, for God's sake, come down."

Jay.

"I can't. Not until I get a guarantee that the tree won't be felled."

There was silence, then another voice.

"Mum, it's me, I'm frightened."

Of course he'd bring Tierre.

"It's OK, sweetheart," she called. "I'm safe here."

If she went down they would arrest her and the tree might be felled that day.

"Mum please." The tone more urgent.

Ash remembered the fear when her mum was dying, knowing she would never see her or hear her sing again.

"Mum!"

She must choose between the tree and the daughter who she was so close to, it was as if some of her blood flowed in Tierre's veins and their minds intertwined as they navigated their complex world.

"I'm coming down."

Unwrapping the rope, she began a careful descent to the tree house. She put her hand on the trunk of the oak and said, "I'm sorry we didn't save you, sorry for all the terrible things that humans are doing to you," then she went down the rope to the ground.

Jay was with Tierre; the police were behind them.

He said, "Bloody hell, Ash. We were terrified."

"Sorry."

She hugged them both. Two officers, a man and a woman, stepped forward.

"We're arresting you for obstruction. Come with us please."

Tierre was crying. "Will you go to prison?"

"No. I'll be back soon, I promise," she said in a firm voice, trying to stop herself from shaking.

They put handcuffs on her, which hurt. She was led away and put in the back seat of the police car; there was a sense of unreality, as if she was an actor in a crime drama. As she was driven away, she smiled at Tierre and Jay and took a last look at the oak, trying to keep the image in her head.

*

They took away her phone and put her in a cell. It had a small window, a rectangle of blue sky and a smell of concrete, mixed with bleach. There was a toilet in one corner, which she used, avoiding looking in the bowl.

Her muscles were trembling. She sat on the hard bed. Exhausted but stretched like a wire. It was cold, as if the sun never reached the room – she zipped up her thin jacket and hugged herself. After a while she lay on the bed and stared at the ceiling. There was a small spider in one corner; she watched as it hung motionless, flyless. She tried to put her mind on positive things, finding a rare moth at the reserve, Tierre jumping over waves, white chalk paths snaking over the hills, in late summer lined with pink and purple marjoram. She wished she had a book.

After what seemed like hours, she heard footsteps and a key in the lock.

"Do you want a cup of tea?" a policeman asked, a soft Yorkshire accent.

"Yes please, no milk. Can I have some water too?"

The tea when it came was lukewarm and stewed but she drank it, and the water. He didn't ask if she wanted anything to eat.

She lay down again. Shut her eyes – what came into her mind was the machine with the huge jaws. She wanted to scream but knew she mustn't, so she stood up and shook, trying to shake off the fear and grief; anyone watching might just think she was cold. She didn't want them to believe she was mad. The light changed in the blue square of window. The spider didn't move.

Much later the door was unlocked again. The same policeman. "You're free to go."

"What will happen?"

"You'll be notified if the police want to pursue the case."

They told her she was lucky that there was no damage. If any of them went back to the camp they'd be charged.

Her phone had run out of battery so she couldn't call Jay. She had some money but there was no phone box. The police station was two and a half miles from her house – it wasn't on a bus route, so she began walking. Passing a local shop, she bought a sandwich and a bottle of water.

Closer to home she came to a fork in the road. She could take the turning that led past the woods, or she could take the other route, which was shorter and meant she'd avoid seeing where the tree had been. She hovered for a moment trying to decide, then chose the longer route.

After another half a mile she came to the track entrance. She could see the wood but not where the oak should be, which was obscured by the hedge.

Although she knew it would break her heart she had to go and look.

Trudging along the sun-hardened mud her stomach was churning and her arms and legs were aching. The view opened up and her heart jumped. She was expecting to see a gap where the tree had been but there was none.

The oak was still there.

She shook her head to clear her vision, in case tiredness and stress had caused her to imagine it, but the scene was the same. She ran across the last part of the field, looked up into the branches of the oak, knowing it's shape intimately, seeing that it was unharmed. She put her hand on the trunk, felt warmth where the sun had been, feeling its power and strength. The roots still ran underneath her feet, Mum's ashes were still merged with the soil. She leaned against the trunk, emotions flooding through her body, relief, exhaustion, grief, joy.

There was a shout and she turned. "Mum!"

Tierre was running across the field, Jay following behind.

Ash opened her arms wide and her daughter ran into them.

"We went to the police station, but they said you'd gone."

Jay caught up. "Why didn't you call?"

"My battery died. The tree's still here – I don't understand."

"After they'd arrested you, a lawyer arrived with an injunction to say that work needed to stop. The boss was furious and tried to argue but the guy had the paperwork. Turns out Oliver Harrison hired him. The bats are too significant to be moved."

"That's amazing."

"It was just in time to stop them felling it."

"I think Clara, the girl in the painting, helped to save it," Tierre said.

"She did and so did Sheila, Hazel, Fly, Dora, you and me, Dad and everyone."

They heard calling. Gavin was cycling across the field.

"And Gavin. If he hadn't let me in the barn, I'd never have known about the bats."

He skidded to a halt. "We're not leaving now. Mum and Dad are pissed off, but I'm happy." He did a wheelie, laughing.

"That's great," Ash said.

"You can come cycling with us at the weekend if you want, can't he, Dad?" Tierre said.

"Sure."

Clouds were moving across the sky, blue had become grey, she felt the first drops of rain; they stood in the open field, soaking up the delicious coolness.

15

The wildlife trust held discussions with the bat trust to work out if they could buy the barn from the Fullers and save it as a permanent roost. The road building was suspended; it seemed unlikely it would ever restart. Netherley wrote an article for the local paper saying he was disgusted by the actions of the small group of disruptive activists and appearing to cast doubt on the importance of Greater Horseshoe Bats.

"He's just bitter because he didn't get his precious bypass," Jay said.

They never found out whether the grey van had anything to do with the fire or their eviction, but Netherley was made Home Secretary, the job he'd been angling for. His association with violent bailiffs hadn't prevented his promotion. In an interview he said he'd be cracking down on eco-protestors.

To celebrate their success Ash and Dora decided to organise a party, and they invited everyone who'd helped save the tree and some who hadn't. They made cake, quiche and salad. It was a chance for the two of them to talk about their experience.

"Thanks for being there and reminding me we were doing the right thing when I had doubts," Ash said.

"It was important and meaningful to me; it helped me realise that I'm capable of changing things. I'm going to keep fighting for Holly and everyone who's affected by air pollution."

The Whispering Oak stood strong and proud, nourished by the rain, decorated with the fabric bunting that Tierre and Maya had helped to make.

Mrs Burnett arrived with her son. "Thanks to you I can stay with my birds," she said. "I was so worried about them. I know they're wild creatures, but they mean so much."

Hazel dropped by on her way to a meeting. "It was interesting being arrested. I've been told by the bishop that I can't ever do anything like that again, but we'll see." She smiled.

Paula, who lived next door to Ash, came. She'd originally supported the bypass. "You went a long way to save the tree, I'm impressed. I've changed my mind about the road, we can do without it. Mmm, this is delicious," she said, as she ate a piece of the cake that Dora had made.

Michael Lester arrived from London. He was still thin but said he was gaining strength. "What you've all done here, Ash, is so important, it may seem like a small battle but it's part of a wider struggle to protect the natural world."

They chatted and ate, listened while Fly sang songs about the wonder of trees. Tierre, Maya and Gavin climbed up to the platform and held their own party.

When it was over, Fly, Dora and Ash dismantled it.

The three of them resolved to stay in touch.

"After what happened at Brooke Wood it's great to remember that sometimes we win," Fly said.

"I loved being here, Ash, it made me feel alive. I don't know what's next but there's something, I can feel it," Dora said.

*

Oliver Harrison hadn't made the party, so Ash went to his house. There were boxes on the living room floor and the bookshelves were empty.

"Have a seat." He pointed to a chair.

Bella lay at her feet.

"Are you leaving?"

"I'm going to stay with my daughter in Guildford. She has a house in the middle of town but at least it has a garden."

"Even though the road isn't going ahead?"

"I'm lonely, I realised. I had a fall last week. I couldn't get up at first, it scared me. Much of my life I wanted to be alone but now…" he shrugged… "night after night. The wildlife is no longer a substitute for human company."

"I wanted to thank you for funding the lawyer."

"I did it for the horseshoe bats. We can't have those wonderful creatures being sacrificed just because some people want to knock a few minutes off a car journey. It's criminal. We all need to do something; you have energy and will, I have money."

"I love that it was bats that saved it. And it felt symbolic too, as if the tree was the world and the people who came together to protest were the population. Maybe one day all our small actions will expand and merge into one."

"I will probably die quite soon but I've lived a long and privileged life and if I help the bats to survive, I'm happy."

Ash said goodbye, sad that she'd probably never see him again – although she hardly knew him, she felt they'd made a connection.

*

Soon after, they went to Cornwall, stayed in a cottage on the very edge of the land, walked the coast path, looking out for whales and basking sharks, Tierre's passion.

"One day, you'll see them," Ash said.

On the day Tierre turned thirteen they made a picnic and headed down the steep path to a small pebble cove for a swim. Ash watched as Tierre dived through a wave. She thought of her mum, who would have loved her – they were similar, slight, dark wavy hair, green eyes.

Tierre came running back with a long strand of seaweed and wrapped it around Jay. He tried to escape, laughing, but she was too fast. They ate sandwiches and birthday cake, explored rock pools looking for crabs, sea anemones and limpets.

In the early hours, unaccustomed to the sounds of the wind making the rafters creak, Ash woke with a start, worrying about Tierre. She got up and went into the other bedroom. Her daughter was lying with one arm flung out, her cheeks were pink. Ash stood watching her – Tierre was alive, happy; she was thankful.

*

In October Dora called to tell Ash about the launch of a new climate group. They promised to do things differently to other NGO's, vowing to make the government act on rising carbon emissions and increasing temperatures.

"I'm signing up. I've been reading about what's going to happen if we don't change direction. Why don't you come with me to see what it's about?"

Ash asked Jay to go with her. She thought he'd dismiss the idea; say he was going cycling or needed to work but he said yes. Since the reunion with his mum something had shifted; he seemed happier and more willing to engage with the world.

They met on the grass opposite the Houses of Parliament, sat on a wall and listened to the speeches. The young Swedish girl was there, the one who held a lone climate strike every Friday. There were pink, yellow and green flags, decorated with a symbol of an egg timer within a circle, time running out. Some people carried placards with powerful images and slogans. There was determination, anger and passion in the air. The speakers said they weren't going to remain silent and watch while the situation worsened.

The declaration was read out, starting with "Tell the Truth."

A call came to lie in the road. They looked at each other, hesitated for a moment, smiled and then went to join the others.

About the Author

Emma Cameron lives with her partner, Rob, in Worthing, West Sussex.

A textile artist and painter for many years, she began writing fiction in 2007.

Her first novel was published under a pseudonym, the second, 'A Scattering', published in 2021.

She is a climate activist, loves rewilding the garden and walking on the South Downs.